EMILY
CHERRY POPPING DADDIES
BOOK I

GOLDEN ANGEL

Cover art by Wicked Smart Designs
Cover Photo taken by CJC Photography
Cover Models: Kevin R. Davis and Emilie Beining

To Meghan Katowitz
Emily's #1 Fan
Thank you so much for all your constant support!!!!!

ACKNOWLEDGEMENTS

Thank you to my backers for this book!

Nessa
Tamie Hartman
Krys Fenner
Kathryn Barr
Judy L.
Barbra
Keema Osbourne
Lynn G.
Ash J.
Connie G.
Joe Kendall
Shavonne Belford

Wendy Martinez
Sheila
Christy R.
Heather Brooks
Gracella
Debi Kiley
Elissa
Angel
JD
Shannon E.
Kiki Clark
Tiffany Walton

Katie Slagle

And an extra big thank you to my Super Backers for this book!

Julie Cole
Nicole
Ceiara
Rhonda Butterbaugh
Karen
Amy Wendt
Katherine
Dalene Schrier
Demaree Holland
Marya
Tracy Honings

Dana Smith
Nadine Berger-Hunter
Brie
Makayla LaLonde
Michell'e M.
Mary Kate Lindquist
Jessica Dempsey
April L.
Jacqueline Larson
Nese
Ilana Jayne

Jennifer Greenberg, LICSW, LCSW-C, CST-S

THE WORST DAY

EMILY

"**Y**ou're fired!"

"What?" All the blood drained from Emily's face as she stared at Ron, the manager who had been harassing her for months. She put up with his leers, his barely veiled innuendos, and his occasional accidental touches, all because she desperately needed this job. She couldn't be fired.

"You heard me." He smirked at her. "You're fired. We don't have enough hours for you."

Still holding her apron, which she'd just taken off, she felt her hands start to shake. She'd just finished a double shift, and she was scheduled for another one tomorrow. Which she didn't mind because it meant that she could eat two staff meals at the diner, saving her a lot of money. She got most of her meals from the diner. Without a job...

"But I'm on the schedule!"

Ron shrugged, his smirk growing into a leer as his gaze traveled up and down her body, lingering on her curves. She had plenty of them. While she might not eat enough at home, subsisting on mostly restaurant meals and noodles meant she kept the frame she'd inherited from her mother.

"If you want to convince me to keep you on..." He let his voice trail off, his hand moving over his body down to his crotch. Emily felt tears spring to her eyes, and she pressed her lips together to keep her sob in her throat. Every part of her body ached, her feet felt like they were twice their normal size, she smelled like grease, and he wanted...

I should just do it. The thought was born out of despair. What other option did she have?

They were in the back hallway, right near the manager's office. Definitely not how Emily imagined losing her virginity. Maybe she could offer him a blow job instead? Not that she'd ever given anyone one of those, either. There was a small part of her that still wanted to hold on to the dream of romance and gentleness and... and... something *more*.

Definitely something more than losing it to a serial

sexual harasser. She didn't know why Ron bothered her. He wasn't bad looking and had a decent body. Women flirted with him all the time. Their clientele all found him charming—so she knew he could be—but for some reason, he got off on bothering her.

And now he was threatening to fire her unless she...

The door to the manager's office opened, making Emily jump. She clutched her apron to her chest, as if she could keep from having to let it—or her job—go as long as she held on to it. Marianne Webster, the owner of the diner, stepped out. It was the first time Emily had ever been glad to see the woman, who was hard as nails and had never smiled once. She insisted on everyone calling her by her first name since this was a 'family establishment,' but that was the closest she came to being friendly.

Petite, grey-haired, and dark-eyed, the woman put her hands on her hips and glared at both Ron and her.

"I don't pay you to stand around gossiping," she snapped at him. Her steely gaze moved to Emily. "Did he tell you we have to let you go?"

The question was a smack in the chest. Emily didn't know what else to do, so she nodded dumbly, her mind completely blank. Her entire world was being upended, and she couldn't even think, much less speak.

"Good. Nothing personal, ya know. I have two nieces who need jobs, and my sister expects me to help them out." Marianne rolled her eyes, shaking her head, but clearly, her sister had won that fight if they were taking Emily's job. "Not enough hours to go around with both of them coming on. If you need a reference, get one from Ron. Ron, get back to work."

With a wave of her hand, Marianne was already turning to walk away. Ron grimaced and skittered past Emily down the hall toward the kitchen. It was only after he brushed past her that she realized he had been trying to get her to do things with him when he clearly had no power over whether or not she kept her job. Asshole.

It didn't matter.

Marianne was the one she needed to talk to.

Shaking off her frozen muscles, Emily darted after the owner, who had just disappeared through the staff door to the parking lot.

"Marianne!" she called out as she pushed the door open.

Almost at her car, which was in the closest parking spot, Marianne turned to look at Emily, lighting up the cigarette hanging from her mouth as she did so. Her eyebrows raised, she tilted her head, the only indication she was waiting for Emily to speak.

"Please, I can't lose this job completely. There have to be some hours I can pick up——"

Shaking her head, Marianne put her palm up to stop Emily.

"No can do. With two of them coming on, there's not going to be any hours left, and there are no other open positions here. Sorry." The apology sounded completely insincere, especially as it was made while Marianne was getting in the car. "Go in and tell the cook that I said you could take a meal home. Don't forget to put Ron down if you need a reference for your next job."

Hope died as Marianne slammed the door behind her, only taking a moment before peeling out of the parking lot. Not that Emily had had much hope left. Closing her eyes, she took deep breaths through her nose, so she didn't start crying in the parking lot.

She still had to go back in and get the food Marianne had offered. There was no way she could turn that down, even though it meant possibly running into Ron again. She also had no illusions about what kind of reference he would give her if she asked him for one.

Pushing back her tears, she wiped away the bit of wetness clinging to her eyelashes and turned on her heel to go back into the restaurant. She would get her meal, and tonight, she would start looking for a new job. Surely, there had to be something out there. Maybe even something better. Without a creepy manager.

Just keep telling yourself that.

Even the voice in her head sounded sarcastic.

DAMIAN

The bus came to a stop right outside the trailer park's entrance. The window above the sink in his trailer had a perfect view of both the entrance and the bus stop, which he liked because that meant he could keep track of who was coming into the neighborhood. His daughter called him a control freak, and she wasn't wrong. But he had his reasons.

When he saw the young woman get off the bus, his shoulders relaxed, and he dropped his head back down to scrub the dish he was cleaning. Did it make sense he'd waited until hours after dinner to do his dishes? Not really. But a little soak never hurt anything. And it allowed him to keep an eye on the bus stop when Emily was due home.

His daughter's best friend—as well as his former

best friend's daughter—he'd known Emily for most of her life. He watched out for her, the same way he did for his own daughter.

Not quite the same way.

A little muscle in his jaw popped as he clenched it and tried to push the lascivious thought out of his mind. At some point, Emily had grown up into a beautiful young woman, and well, Damian had turned into a dirty old man, lusting after a woman far too young for him. It was gross, dirty, perverted, and wrong, but he couldn't get her out of his head.

While he might not be able to control his thoughts, he could control his actions. So, he kept his distance while also keeping an eye on her. Looking up again, he frowned when he saw the way she was clutching a bag to her chest. It couldn't be that she was cold. The weather was balmy tonight, a little humid even, and she was wearing a short-sleeve shirt and pants that were perfectly appropriate.

With her long fall of hair half-covering her face, he couldn't see much of her expression, especially in the streetlights. Frowning, he put down the dish he was washing and leaned forward, as if those few inches would make any real difference in what he could see.

The trailer she lived in, the one that technically still belonged to her parents, was a couple blocks past his. He didn't worry once she was in the trailer park, though. She was safe here. Damian made sure to both know his neighbors and ensure they knew who he was. He avoided Emily's trailer, but he felt assured no one was going to mess with her there.

They all watched out for each other.

As evidenced by the text that came through ten minutes later from Mrs. Martine, letting him know that Emily had gotten home. The older woman, who lived a little down the block from Emily, kept him updated. In return, he did odd handyman jobs for her, which meant he didn't end up stalking Emily home every night. So, everyone was happy.

Then a second text came through—Mrs. Martine thought Emily looked upset.

Which confirmed what he'd thought. She would have gotten a better look at Emily than he'd managed. Frowning, he quickly finished washing his dishes and glanced at the clock. It wasn't too late to call his daughter. Katrina had received her bachelor's degree last year and decided to get to work on her master's, which she was doing on the west coast, so she was three hours behind him and Emily.

She answered on the second ring.

"Hello, Father." The rolling way she said the formal greeting made it sound almost mocking. Damian rolled his eyes.

"Hey, sweetie, how are you? How's school?" He couldn't jump right into asking about Emily. Along with being way too young for him, he would never do anything to risk the girls' relationship. If he'd still been friends with Emily's father, he wouldn't have done anything to risk that relationship, either, but Don had ruined their friendship all on his own.

Still, that wasn't Emily's fault.

Making the appropriate noises and nodding as his daughter regaled him with how well she was doing, Damian bided his time, keeping tight reins on his patience.

"How's everything at home?" she finally asked him.

"Good, good. Work's been good. All the shops have been good." He owned several scattered throughout the county. Good mechanics were valued. In his own shop, his guys handled the day-to-day jobs while he focused on his specialty—restoring the classics. It was often both fun and frustrating work, as well as being lucrative. "I have a Ferrari coming in later this week that I'll be restoring." He didn't bother giving her the specs. He knew she didn't care about that. Sadly, his love of cars had not passed on to his daughter.

"Oh, fun." Despite having no interest of her own, she did her best to sound enthused because she knew he was happy about it. Damian couldn't help but grin. "How are Uncle Desmond and Uncle Braden?"

He rolled his eyes, even though she couldn't see it. She always asked after her uncles.

"Uncle Braden's doing great. Keeping busy." In fact, he hadn't seen his brother in a week or so. He should probably reach out and see if Braden wanted to do dinner.

"And Uncle Desmond?" Now, her voice had definitely taken on a teasing note.

"You've probably talked to him more recently than I have." Which was a sad state of affairs but also the truth. Sometimes, brothers just didn't get along. Though it would help if Desmond could pull the stick out of his ass. He cleared his throat. "So, speaking of people at home, have you heard from Emily lately?"

"Daaaaad." Katrina drawled out the word, laden with complaint. "Please tell me you aren't butting your nose into everyone's business again."

"It's a simple question, Katrina." He drummed his fingers on the countertop. "Mrs. Martine texted me and said she thought Emily seemed upset when she came home tonight. I haven't talked to her recently, but I thought maybe you had."

"Uh-huh, blame Mrs. Martine." His daughter's

dry tone told him she wasn't buying it. "You aren't the whole park's dad, you know."

"It's not a bad thing to be a concerned neighbor."

"Okay, Trailer Park Daddy. You know there's such a thing as being *too* neighborly, right?" she asked, before he could object to the nickname. "I'll talk to Emily and make sure she's okay. You can tell *Mrs. Martine* I've got it handled."

"Thanks, pumpkin, I'll be sure to do that." Even though it didn't give him the sense of satisfaction he needed. While he trusted his daughter to do right by her friend, there was a part of him that wanted to be the one to find out what was going on with Emily... because if something was wrong, then he could fix it for her.

What he really didn't want to tell his daughter was that she was hitting a little too close to home with the 'Daddy' remark. Those were needs he'd buried a long time ago when he'd buried his wife. And thinking about himself as a Daddy when it came to Emily...

Yeah, he needed to get his mind off that real fast.

"Do you need anything?" he asked, changing subjects to something much safer. "Did I give you enough of an allowance for the month?"

"I'm fine, dad. You gave me more than enough. Just like last year. I've got a savings account now, thanks to you." Katrina sounded amused, but there was also real appreciation in her voice. "I'm concentrating on school, just like you want me to. I'm going to be looking for a part-time position this year, though, so I don't graduate with my master's and no experience."

"Oh, right, that's probably good." Though, if she needed it, he would keep helping her out after she graduated. Living the way he did while owning several businesses meant his savings account was robust, and he had plenty of investments on top of that. He kept his wealth pretty quiet because he'd seen how money could change people, and he was satisfied with how he lived. Eventually, it would all go to Katrina, and that was all he really cared about.

"Alright, I have to go, especially if I'm going to call Emily tonight. Love you, Dad."

"Love you too, sweetie. Have a good night." He bit back a request to let him know how her conversation with Emily went. He already knew what the answer would be, and it might raise suspicions and thoughts he definitely did not want her to have.

"Night."

Damian hung up the phone and stared out at the bus stop, tapping his fingers on the counter. He still felt unsatisfied, but he'd done all he could do.

2

THE LIES

EMILY

Standing at her kitchen table, Emily sniffled, taking out the boxes of food the cooks had given her. Thankfully, Ron had been in the dining room when she'd gone into the kitchen with her request, and they'd loaded her down as much as they could. The two boxes of rolls could be frozen, and that would give her something to eat for the next couple weeks. They'd also given her the family-size containers of mac'n'cheese and potato salad.

The pasta would freeze better, so she'd do that and eat the potato salad this week, along with the fresh fruit and the mixed green salad. The greens were almost always part of the family meal, but the fresh fruit was a luxury she didn't often get to indulge in. Even though the strawberries were a little overripe and the peaches were a bit bruised, she was going to enjoy eating them.

She couldn't even drown her tears in a vat of ice cream. She couldn't remember the last time she'd been able to afford any, so she'd be crying into her fruit salad instead. It was the one small, nice thing she could do for herself on this especially shitty night.

She'd just gotten everything put away and her fresh fruit sliced and put in a bowl when her phone rang.

Katrina.

Her best friend, who was living the life Emily desperately wished for. But she couldn't be mad at Katrina just because she'd been able to go to college and was now getting her master's. Katrina was just really lucky. They'd never talked about it, but Emily figured her friend must have gotten a bunch of scholarships to be able to go to school all the way across the country. That or she was going to be drowning in student loan debt after she graduated. They didn't talk about money, though. No one did in their neighborhood.

She missed Katrina like crazy, but part of her was glad she didn't have to see her friend too often.

Knowing Katrina was out there going to college while Emily was still stuck here... well, it hurt.

But she could use her best friend tonight, even if it meant admitting she'd gotten fired from a job she couldn't afford to lose.

"Hello." She forced as much cheerfulness into her voice as she could, wincing because she realized it hadn't done the trick as soon as she heard herself. It was really obvious she'd been crying, and Katrina picked up on it right away.

"Oh no, what's wrong?"

No beating around the bush for her bestie. God, Emily wished she could be more like Katrina. "I got f-f-fired." Blinking back another assault of tears, Emily barely managed to get the words out.

"What?" Katrina's outrage shook the phone in waves. "What the hell? You're the best worker that shitty diner has!"

"Marianne wants to hire her nieces." Emily hiccuped.

"Fucking nepotism! You should fucking sue them. Hell, if I was there, I'd march right down and—"

"I appreciate that, hun, but it wouldn't get me my job back." Emily interrupted her friend. As much as she appreciated the righteous anger, she didn't have the energy to join it. She mostly wanted to wallow.

"I'm sorry, hun," Katrina said, shifting gears immediately in response to Emily's unvoiced request, her voice full of sympathy. That was the best thing about being lifelong best friends; Katrina knew her so well, she didn't even need to ask. "That really, really sucks. Fuck them. They suck. All of them suck. Marianne especially sucks. She sucks big, fat donkey dong." Some of her anger remained in her ranting, but it had lost the edge.

Despite her roiling emotions, Emily couldn't help a watery giggle. This was why she'd picked up the phone. Despite her deep envy for Katrina's life, her bestie always knew how to make her feel better. She missed her so much. This was one of the times when it sucked that she was all the way across the country.

"Maybe not, but it's not like there are a lot of options around here." Emily sighed, the feeling of total defeat washing over her again.

"Hey, it's been a while since you've looked, right? Maybe there are more now."

Emily sniffled again because, despite Katrina's encouraging tone, they both knew the truth. There just weren't many jobs around them that she could use the bus to get to and that wanted someone with nothing more than a high school diploma. There were also a lot of things Emily hadn't told Katrina because she was too ashamed.

Like how her credit card bills had mounted up,

the high interest making them even bigger every month, even when she didn't use them. Like how she hadn't been able to pay the electricity bill the past two months. Like how she was living off of noodles and the meals at the diner.

If she couldn't get another job that fed her, she didn't know how she was going to afford everything else. More tears welled up in her eyes.

"Right," she said. "I'm gonna start looking tomorrow." Katrina didn't need Emily bringing her down. And she was right. Maybe there would be something.

"And if you need money for anything, I can help you out in the meantime," Katrina said sternly.

"What? No, you can't do that." Emily was flabbergasted. She knew exactly how much college cost. "You're not working, are you?"

"Not yet, but I will be, and I have savings—"

"No." Emily interrupted her with a firm denial. She knew Katrina meant well, but anything she was able to share with Emily would be a mere drop in the bucket, and then she'd owe money to a friend, which was so much worse than owing it to a faceless company. Especially since she wasn't sure she would ever be able to pay it back. There was no way she was going to risk her friendship like that.

"I'm just saying." Katrina sighed with exasperation. "Look, I know it's considered gauche to talk about money, but I can help you."

The only reason she thought she could help was because Emily had deliberately omitted a lot of facts about how bad her situation really was. The familiar feeling of shame flowed through her. She didn't want Katrina to know how bad it was. Didn't want anyone to know.

What she really wanted was to be able to fix it and never have anyone else know how bad it had gotten... unless she was telling them how she'd gotten out of it.

"I'll be okay. I'm going to look for a new job, and I'll get by until then." The food she'd brought home tonight would help with that. Hey, she might even drop a few pounds since she was going to have to ration the food, and none of it was fried. Though that didn't feel like a good thing right now.

"You have to promise me if there's anything you *need*, you'll tell me," Katrina insisted. "I know you. You're the suffer-in-silence type, but I don't want you suffering at all."

Katrina didn't know the half of it. She'd be so pissed off if she did. This was one of the upsides to her bestie living across the country. She had no idea how bad it had gotten for Emily.

"I will, I promise." That was an easy enough

promise to make. She wasn't really lying. She didn't actually *need* anything yet. 'Need' was a very strong word. She'd be fine for now, and... she'd figure things out. She would. Just talking to Katrina helped bolster her determination because she wanted to be able to give her friend good news. "It was a long day, though, and I just want to get to sleep."

"Okay, sweetie. I love you. Take care of yourself."

"Right back at you. Love you." Emily's smile faded after she hung up, and she sighed. Settling down onto the hard wooden chair, she slowly ate her fruit, savoring every sweet bite while doing the very bitter work of scrolling through job sites. She had her resume all queued up and saved in her phone. She'd had to put it together at the library and email it to herself, but it made applying easy... the hard part was getting a response.

Send.

Send.

Send.

It was something she'd done a million times before. She applied to a bunch of listings that all said they required four-year degrees because that was all that was listed on those sites before she went to the online community boards. That's where she'd found her job at the diner. Maybe there were more restaurants hiring.

Her heart sank as she looked at the dearth online. Maybe everyone was doing in-person hiring? But she knew that wasn't true.

Literally, the only listing was for the gentleman's club that was in the next town over, about half an hour away by bus, but the bus did go there.

Gentleman's club. Call a spade a spade—it's a strip club, honey.

Emily stared at the listing, which boasted their young women could make thousands of dollars in one night. Her stomach cramped at the very thought.

I don't know how to strip.

But I do know how to dance.

No one is going to want to watch a virgin stripper.

They're not going to know that I'm a virgin.

I'm a size eighteen. Pretty sure strippers are supposed to be a size zero.

Variety is the spice of life.

I don't want to be a stripper.

She'd only ever had one boyfriend in high school, and he'd dumped her after her mom had been arrested. He hadn't wanted to be in a relationship with the daughter of a junkie who was going to jail. Though, truthfully, Emily sometimes wondered if that had just been the excuse because she'd been putting off sleeping with him. Kirk the Jerk was what Katrina had called him after that.

Trying to imagine herself getting naked in front of one man, much less a bunch of men, made her want to curl into a little ball.

Thousands of dollars in one night.

She'd promised Katrina that she would let her friend know if there was anything she needed. What did it say about her that becoming a virgin stripper seemed easier than asking her best friend for money?

That's if they'd even hire me.

It would be the answer to all her prayers if they did. Plenty of money. She could pay the bills. She could pay off her credit cards. She could get herself back on her feet. It wasn't like it had to be forever.

Sleep on it.

That's what she would do. She would sleep on it... if she could fall asleep.

Pressing her lips together, she went to the bookshelf to pick up the worn-out copy of Stella Moore's *Worthy*. She'd gotten it for a dollar at a used bookstore a year ago and read it about a million times since then. What she wouldn't give to have a hot, rich baseball player come into her life, worship her curves, and take care of her for the rest of her life.

Though she kind of wished he was a Daddy Dom.

Emily had her own fair share of so-called Daddy issues. Having a Daddy Dom who actually cared about her sounded like heaven, but she was pretty sure those didn't exist in real life. Or, if they did, they were all at expensive kink clubs like the one in her book. She'd never get to go there.

❧

DAMIAN

"Oh, Daddy..."

Emily moaned as she squirmed on his lap, her rounded bottom covered in bright pink handprints. Damian's cock throbbed against her soft side as he spanked her again, watching her ass jiggle from the impact of his hand. Putting his hand against her hot flesh, he caressed her cheek while she whimpered, dipping his fingers down between her legs to stroke her wet pussy.

She cried out, bucking her hips up as he plunged his fingers inside her, soaking his hand in her arousal.

"Daddy, please," she begged. "I need you... I need you to fuck me..."

Those were the words that vaulted Damian out of the dream and back into his lonely, cold bed. He'd never actually heard Emily curse in real life.

Waking up fucking sucked. He was hard as a rock. Other than her cursing, the dream had been so fucking real, he could still feel her soft curves pressing against his legs and stomach. Groaning, he reached for his dick, wishing he could banish the image of her from his head.

It wasn't as though he knew what she actually looked like naked. He'd seen her in a bathing suit last summer when Katrina was home, and apparently, that was all his brain needed to extrapolate. Soft, plush curves, a rounded tummy, hips that he could grip, and a perfectly spankable ass...

Fantasizing about her might make him a dirty old man, but now that he'd started, he couldn't stop. He jerked his cock, closing his eyes and letting his imagination run free. Fuck, what he wouldn't give to feel her mouth around his dick, her wide eyes looking up at him, swimming with tears from a spanking while she 'apologized' by taking him into her throat. Her legs spread wide, arms cuffed to his bed, so he could feast on her sweet pussy until she was limp and hoarse from too many orgasms.

Then he'd move up, still holding her legs spread wide, and thrust his cock into her. Kiss her and muffle her cries with his tongue, letting her taste herself on his lips. Fuck her into oblivion while she screamed 'Daddy' as he filled her with his cock, over and over and over...

Damian grunted as his orgasm crested, hot cum splashing over his stomach. He worked his fist, wringing every last bit of pleasure from his dick...

hoping that would be the end of it, that his body and mind would be satisfied.

Now that he thoroughly felt like a dirty old man, he was going to take a shower, then try to get some more shut-eye. Sighing, he forced himself to his feet, grimacing as he glanced down at the white trails of his cum coating his stomach.

He should probably go back to BDE, the kink club he and his brothers co-owned. Sure, he and Desmond were silent partners, letting Braden be the face and run everything, but it meant he could stop in whenever he wanted. He just very rarely wanted to.

There had been a few times over the years after Anita died when he'd gotten so lonely and desperate for the touch of a woman, he'd gone in to find someone for a night. But he hated doing that. Damian had never been a 'one-night' kind of guy. He liked relationships. He liked getting to know a woman before he fucked her.

He also hadn't wanted to take the time to get to know anyone while Katrina was younger. She'd been a lost little girl without her mom, and needed all his attention. Eventually, his attention divided between her and his various businesses as she'd gotten older and more independent. Those businesses allowed him to take care of her in other ways, like putting her through school without racking up any student loan debt.

Which was a good thing because that shit was a fucking racket.

Turning on the water, Damian stepped under the spray, shaking his head as he doused it. The water slid over his skin and hair, soaking into his goatee. It helped clear his head a little. He scrubbed himself down over the tattoos on his chest and arms, focusing on getting himself clean and not thinking about Emily at all.

Nope. He was going to think about a different woman. He didn't have one in mind, but he needed to find one. It was time.

He'd go to BDE, start meeting people, and find someone he could really connect with. He needed to get past this thing he had about Emily. He needed to get it fully in his head that was never going to happen.

3

A DESPERATE AUDITION

EMILY

Victor, as he'd introduced himself when Emily had been shown into his office, looked her over. Oddly, his gaze felt less sleazy than Ron's. If anything, it was clinical. He frowned, leaning back in his chair while she tried not to feel too awkward about standing while he was still sitting.

"*You* want to be a dancer?" he asked doubtfully, his gaze sweeping over her high-necked blouse and knee-length skirt. It was the best Emily could do. It wasn't like she had a ton of clothes for going out and partying—because she didn't—and she never went on dates.

"Yes." Emily said the word as forcefully as she

could, as if she could make herself mean it by saying it more firmly. "I don't have any experience, but I'm a fast learner. Or if you need any servers. I could be a server. Or a bartender. I know how to mix drinks."

Good job. Way to make sure he knows you're desperate.

But there was something about him that made her feel like she could say that, and he wouldn't try to take advantage of her. Not the way Ron had. That jerk.

Victor looked to be in his mid-forties and wasn't anything like what she'd expected when she'd arrived at the club to apply. Firstly, he wasn't giving her a creep vibe. Secondly, he looked like he wanted to talk her out of applying. He was wearing a business suit, though no tie, and he had the collar button undone. There was no hair hanging out of his shirt, though, and no gold chains. The hair on his head was neatly styled and looked as if it might have been blow-dried.

Basically, he didn't look anything like what she'd seen in the movies, and she was realizing she had some ideas about clubs like this that might not be correct.

God, she hoped so.

She could work for a guy like Victor. Sure, her first impression might be completely off, or maybe she was projecting because she was terrified of the alternative—which was not working for anyone at all

—but she did feel a little reassured that maybe this wouldn't be too terrible.

Letting out a hefty sigh, Victor looked her over again.

"We don't need any more servers or bartenders. We need dancers." He eyed her blouse again. "The guys would probably like your curves. You're bigger than most of the girls we get, but that's not necessarily a bad thing. It could be part of your schtick." Suddenly, he stood, the chair creaking as he got to his feet. He was a few inches taller than her, not enough to make her feel intimidated or like he was looming. "Alright, come with me. Let's see what you've got."

"What?" Emily blinked as he came around the desk, passing by her and crooking his finger.

"Let's see what you've got," he repeated, opening the door and stepping back as he gestured for her to walk through in front of him. Now that the door was open, she could hear the music from the restaurant coming down the hall. It wasn't loud, but it was audible, a throbbing bass beat she felt in her suddenly churning gut.

"Does this mean I'm hired?" Trotting along behind him, she felt as though this wasn't real. It had to be a dream. He wasn't just going to hire her when she hadn't filled out any paperwork or anything.

"No, this means you get an audition. Any money

you make is yours." The music was getting louder, the lights dimmer. She could hear the murmur of voices out in the main room now, all low and masculine, and her stomach flip-flopped. Nausea rose in the back of her throat, and she swallowed it back hard.

They stopped in what was clearly a backstage area. The stage was up several stairs, and from her position, she couldn't see the woman who was currently performing, but she could see the lights shining onto the stage. Standing just next to the stairs in the dark was a blonde woman, who seemed to be wearing some sort of shimmery top and shorts, which was the only reason Emily spotted her. The woman was looking at her curiously.

That was the kind of outfit Victor had probably been expecting from anyone coming in for a job.

"An audition?" Her voice came out in a high squeak that she barely recognized. "I... I..."

"Look, honey, I'm not going to hire you if I don't know that you can do the job." Victor put his hands on his hips. "It's not an easy job, but it makes damn good money if you can get it done. It's not a job for everyone. This is the morning crowd. They don't give a shit if you can't dance or if you're awkward when you're taking your clothes off. You get past this, and we'll get you trained up a bit, keep you on the daytime crew until you're a better dancer, then move things around."

Frowning at her, he tilted his head toward the stage. Emily stood frozen in place, unable to speak as he continued.

"The day is when I need someone. It makes the least amount of money, and several of the dancers are ready to move to the evenings if we can find a replacement. But I'm not going to hire you without knowing you can get on stage and take your clothes off. Down to your panties. You can keep those on, though it's probably too much to hope you're wearing a g-string?"

Heat flushing through her face, Emily shook her head. She'd never owned a regular thong, must less a g-string, and right now, that was making her feel even less confident. Even though she'd tried to look nice to come to apply for a job, she hadn't expected an audition.

In the back of her head, she realized she'd been hoping she would either be told 'no' immediately or —worst-case scenario—she'd be hired but need to be trained. She wanted the chance to find another job before actually getting up on stage and taking off her clothes in front of an audience.

Oh no, oh no, oh no...

The music died to scattered applause. Emily

jumped as another woman suddenly appeared at the back of the stage and came down. She was almost completely naked, except for a barely there red-mesh thong that was completely see-through. It matched her fire-engine hair. Fabric hung from one hand, probably the clothes she'd had on before she'd started stripping.

"Hold on, Cassie. Emily is going to go up first for an audition," Victor said to the blonde. The redhead paused, now also staring at Emily, who felt like her cheeks were so hot, they must be visible in the darkness.

"Okay, go get 'em, girl," the blonde said. She even sounded sincere.

Oh God.

What choice did she have? None, really. She needed a job. She needed money. She was out of options.

Forcing one foot in front of the other, Emily swallowed hard as she stepped up the stairs.

"Faster, sunshine," Victor snapped out.

Something about the authoritative order helped her move faster, and she suddenly found herself at the top of the stairs at the back of the stage.

The bright lights hit her, hot and blinding... but not nearly as blinding as she wished because when she blinked, she could see out into the restaurant. It was not nearly as empty as she might have hoped. There were quite a few men scattered among the tables, and—worse—seven of them right up against the edge of the stage.

She could see their faces. Their leers.

"Dance!" Victor yelled from backstage. There was a part of her that recognized that he was trying to help her out, but this time, the command didn't work. She froze.

How the hell had she thought she'd be able to do this? She'd never gotten naked in front of *any* man before. Tears clogged her throat, and she took a step back. One of the men started jeering.

"Take off your clothes, ice queen!"

"She sucks. Where's Cassie?"

"Move, fattie!"

Choking on her tears, Emily dashed off the stage, the taunts of the men ringing in her ears. As she ran off, Cassie ran on, and she could hear the cheers over the music as the pretty blonde came out on stage.

At the bottom of the stairs, the redhead was still there, mostly naked, with a sympathetic expression, while Victor shook his head as if he'd known it all along. Emily's knees buckled, and she sat down heavily on the bottom of the stairs, tears streaming down her cheeks as she pressed her hand against her pounding heart.

"I don't think this is the job for you, sunshine," he said.

"Why did you send her up there like that?" the redhead asked, giving him a mean look. "You can tell she's never stripped before."

"To show her that she's not going to be able to do the job." Victor sounded exasperated. "I don't think she had any idea what she was getting into. Now she knows. Come on, sunshine. Let's get you out of here."

"Oh my god, Victor, give her a minute. Here, I'll stay with her. You go do whatever it is you need to do." The redhead waved him off, and after a second glance at Emily, who couldn't meet his gaze, he left. Sitting down next to Emily, the redhead rubbed her back. "Deep breaths, sweetie. That's it. One more. Now, let it out slowly. Good. So, my name is Penny. What's your name?"

"Emily." She managed to get her name out, though it still felt as if she was choking. The back rub and sympathy helped, as did the deep breaths, but she was distracted by the naked boobs swaying so close to her arm. She supposed casual nudity wasn't a big deal after getting undressed on a stage.

Victor was right. She didn't think this was the job for her. The courage it must take to get up there and get naked under all those leering, judgmental eyes... desperation apparently wasn't enough. She'd frozen.

Maybe if she tried again now that she knew what it would be like? But just the idea of going back up there made her want to break down sobbing. Knowing what it would be like made it worse, not better. Ignorance had been bliss.

"Why do you want to be a dancer, Emily?"

"I don't." Emily hiccupped. "I've never gotten naked in front of anyone before, other than my best friend. But I got fired yesterday, and it seems like no one else is hiring, and I'm desperate, and—"

"Woah, wait, you've never gotten naked in front of anyone else?" Penny's back rub paused. "So, you're like, a virgin?"

Emily nodded. Penny let out a low whistle and started rubbing circles on Emily's back again. It felt nice. Almost motherly. God, she missed her mom. Not that she would ever tell her mom that she'd tried to apply to work at a strip club. Her mom had enough guilt, being stuck in prison and knowing how Emily was struggling without either of her parents to help her.

Like Katrina, Emily's mom didn't know exactly how bad things had gotten. There was nothing she could do, after all, and Emily didn't want to add to her burden.

Plus, she hoped that by the time her mom was out, she'd have her life together.

"Okay, this isn't the place to talk. Come with me. Maybe I can help you out." Penny patted Emily's back. Not knowing what else to do, Emily got to her feet and followed Penny down the hall to a door that led into a dressing room. There were two other women in there, both getting ready for their turn on the stage. They blinked in surprise when they saw Emily.

"Hey, Sasha, I need you to tell this chick about that virgin auction your friend did."

"Virgin auction?" Emily asked, startled. She took a step back toward the door they'd just come through.

Penny spun around and gave Emily a hard look.

"You're desperate, right? And a virgin. You need money, and I don't think you're cut out to be a stripper. The auction will get you a lot more money than stripping, and you'll only have to get naked in front of one person. Plus, some guy who's willing to pay to pop a cherry isn't going to mind a bit of crying."

She summed up the situation so matter-of-factly, Emily couldn't think of a single argument. It was like her mind had gone completely blank.

"Let me guess, you were thinking your first time would be special," said the woman who came to stand next to Penny. Sasha, presumably. Long black hair flowed over her shoulders and down to her waist, half-covering the bikini she was wearing. Behind her, the other woman was seated in front of the mirror, twisting her dreadlocks into a complicated knot on top of her head, seemingly disinterested in the conversation.

Rather than answering, Emily looked at the floor. Because, yeah, she had wanted it to be special. Romantic. But Penny was right. She was running out of options.

"Trust me, a couple hundred thousand dollars, and it will feel real special," Sasha said with a snicker.

Emily's jaw dropped.

"A couple hundred thousand dollars?" she asked faintly.

"Yeah. I mean, you can't *expect* that, but that's what my friend Lacey got." Sasha shrugged. "This particular auction guarantees at least fifty thousand because you have to be willing to do more than just sex. The clients are all vetted, and they're not allowed to do anything that would cause permanent marks or harm you or anything. Lacey got tied up and spanked, did some oral, then got fucked for the first time and earned a couple hundred thousand. One night and all that money. I wanted to sign up, but my boyfriend said no." She sighed.

"You're a virgin?" Emily blinked, not sure whether she was more surprised by that or hearing that Sasha had a boyfriend who was apparently okay with stripping but not with selling her virginity. Though... they were two very different things when she took a moment to think about it.

Sasha laughed so hard, she bent over.

Emily blushed. Not a virgin, then. She'd misunderstood.

"No, no," Sasha wiped tears away from her eyes as she straightened. Behind her, Penny and the black girl were laughing, too, not bothering to hide their mirth. "Oh God, that's the funniest thing I've heard all day. I'm not a virgin, but the auction is for selling fantasies. Whatever you want. I figured someone's gotta have a fantasy about fucking a stripper, and I could make some money. Virgins tend to get the best prices, though, since that's something you can only do once. I probably wouldn't get more than a hundred thousand, but that would be worth it for one night." She sighed.

It sounded almost too good to be true. One night, one small thing and all her problems would be solved. She didn't have anyone special to give it to anyway. Penny had been right, too—it would be easier with one man. It had to be, right?

❧ 4 ☙

IT'S TIME

DAMIAN

Leaning against the grave, Damian sighed and patted the ground where Anita lay. It had been close to twenty years, and he still missed her. The purple tulips he'd laid on the headstone were her favorite, and he tried to make it by at least a couple times a month to replace them. In the beginning, he'd come by almost every day, then it had become every week, and now it was a couple times a month. Sometimes, only once a month.

"Sorry, baby," he murmured. "It's not that I don't want to see you. It's just... life."

He could almost hear her laugh in his head, see her flashing brown eyes as she grinned at him. Anita had always been the easygoing one, the one who flowed with what was happening around them. She would have told him not to worry because it wasn't like it made a difference to her whether or not he visited. When they got the cancer diagnosis, she'd been the one to tell him she wanted him to move on and find happiness.

You'll get to have two wives in heaven. Maybe I'll see if I can find a second husband up there, too. That way, we both have to share.

"It's time, Anita. You'd probably tell me it was past time. I'm going to finally get out there and try to find... something. I don't know if it'll be a second wife, but I know you'd be pissed as hell at me for putting aside my own wants and needs for so long." He ran his fingers through the grass, his chest aching as he spoke. He knew it was all in his head, but he often felt as though she was really listening when he did this. Like wherever she was, she could hear him.

"I just wanted to raise Katrina right. I'm pretty sure you'd have told me I could do that *and* have a dating life, but I wasn't so sure. But she's all grown up now. You'd be so proud."

Tipping his head back, he stared up at the sky. Though he couldn't feel the wind, he could see the clouds moving across the clear blue. For a long moment, he watched them. With such a big damn universe, his problems felt so tiny.

"I'm going to BDE tonight. I don't know if I'll find someone there, but I know I need to start looking." He hesitated, but if he couldn't tell Anita, who could he tell? "I've been having inappropriate thoughts about Emily. Remember Don and Elizabeth? That would be their daughter. You only got to meet her once when she was a baby. Yeah, the same age as our daughter, and if some old asshole my age was having the kind of thoughts about Katrina that I've been having about Emily..."

He'd fucking kill the man.

Probably.

Make sure our daughter has a happy life.

That was one of the last things Anita ever said to him. Make sure Katrina has a happy life. And if she came home with a boyfriend that was Damian's age, but who made her happy?

Go-with-the-flow Anita would have gone with it. Damian sighed. She'd probably talk him down from kicking the guy's ass and into accepting him because it made Katrina happy. But that didn't mean *he* wasn't a dirty fucking pervert. He could only imagine what Don and Elizabeth would think if they found out he was lusting after their daughter.

Scratch that. He didn't give a fuck what Don

thought. The asshole had turned into a complete piece of trash over the years. Damian had held onto the friendship because Don had been such a support to him after Anita died, but eventually, even he couldn't keep putting up with the toxic shit that spewed from Don's mouth. He'd somehow gone from being a decent guy with occasional asshole tendencies to being a racist, homophobic, misogynistic piece of crap, then he'd started drinking and gambling on top of it. When he'd gambled away his trailer, it had been Damian who stepped in and saved him—not for Don, but for Elizabeth and Emily.

Unfortunately, that had just left Don free to start gambling again. Then he'd gotten pissed at Elizabeth for trying to stop him, cheated on her left and right, and eventually, she'd ended up turning to drugs to help her through her life. Don had turned her in, retaliating when she wouldn't hand over her paycheck. Something Damian was reasonably sure Emily still didn't know, but Elizabeth had told him when he'd paid for her lawyer.

So, yeah. Fuck Don. There was still a part of Damian that instinctively cared what his old friend would have thought... but that old friend was long gone and had turned into someone else completely.

He still cringed when he thought about Elizabeth. He'd visited her a few times and kept in touch with her after she was sent to prison. Trying to picture her reaction to hearing her loser husband's former best friend was with her daughter?

Yeah, no. Fuck that. He couldn't imagine that going over well in any scenario, no matter how open-minded a person was. He still felt guilty for not having done more for her, even though he wasn't sure what else he might have been able to do.

"Anyway." He leaned his head against the cool stone. "I'm going to BDE tonight. I need to get Emily out of my head so I can stop feeling like such a pervert. Find a date who's age-appropriate. Someone I can have a future with."

After another long moment, he patted the grass again and straightened up.

"I've gotta go. I'll be back, though. I promise I won't forget to visit, even if I do start dating and even if I ever get a second wife." He didn't intend to ever make Katrina feel like he'd pushed her mom out of the way in favor of someone else.

Heading back to his garage, his lunch break over, he waved to his workers on his way in.

"Hey boss, that part you were waiting for arrived," Brad, one of his techs, called over to him as he passed.

"Thanks." Damian nodded his acknowledgment

and picked up his pace a bit. Losing himself in work right now felt like a good thing.

჻

EMILY

The auction website was everything Sasha said it would be. Emily used the password Sasha had given her to get in and look around. There were all sorts of people—not just women—of all shapes, sizes, races, and ages. If someone had a fantasy they wanted fulfilled, they'd be able to do it there.

Some of the descriptions of what the participants were offering made her cringe.

There was a whole section for virgins but only two listings under it. That meant there wasn't a lot of competition, which meant more money. Maybe because there weren't that many virgins around the area. At least, not ones who were over eighteen.

The next auction was on Friday.

If she wanted in, she needed to get herself uploaded onto the site by midnight tonight, which didn't leave her much time to decide. At least she'd been able to go to the library today to use their wi-fi, so she could upload her application through her phone—if she decided to go through with it. Hopefully, she didn't introduce a virus or something into their system, but... she didn't have many other options. She was going to run out of data before the end of the month if she didn't keep a careful eye on it, then where would she be? The library was the best place for her to get free wi-fi.

Scrunching herself back farther against the book-shelf, Emily lifted her head to look around again, even though no one would be able to see the screen of her phone since she was in a corner. She still felt like she was doing something wrong.

Scrolling through the site, Emily pressed her lips together. Looking actually made her feel a little better. Some people showed their faces in the photos, some didn't. Some had their faces cropped out or were wearing some kind of mask. That appealed to her. A mask would be good because then she couldn't be recognized.

Which was a possibility that hadn't occurred to her until she'd been looking at the site and recognized one of the women offering a 'night of being humiliated and verbally tortured.' Emily didn't know much about her other than her name was Amanda, and she liked to dunk her pickles in her tomato juice. The fact that she'd recognized anyone had taken her aback even more than what Amanda was offering.

Not that she used her real name. According to the

description, Mistress Avery only offered verbal humiliation and torment. There would be no sexual contact whatsoever.

If only that was possible for her... but the guaranteed income from what Mistress Avery was offering was a lot lower than what a virgin would get. Emily had found the guarantees in the application section. A lot of them were kind of general, but enough for her to get the idea that virgins were a big draw.

Plus, there wasn't much she could do to fulfill someone's fantasy without sex, which meant she'd be giving it up, anyway.

A couple hundred thousand dollars would make it feel real special. Sasha hadn't been wrong.

Her romantic prospects were nonexistent. Who had she been saving it for? Maybe the reason she'd never had sex wasn't because the universe was going to send her someone special, but now she could use it to get her life back on track. Money might not buy happiness, but at this point, she would settle for security. It wasn't as if she could even think about being happy when she was very likely to end up on the streets, starving, if she didn't do something to fix her situation now.

Why not use her virginity to fix her life?

It wasn't doing her any other kind of good.

Then she'd never have to admit to Katrina how

bad it had gotten. Never have to admit it to her mom. No one would ever need to know. How would they know? They wouldn't.

Am I really going to do this?

Do I really have another choice?

She could always go back to the strip club and beg Victor to give her another chance, but did she really have the guts to try again, even if he agreed? Sasha had had a point about only having to get naked in front of one guy. Plus, since he'd paid for her, it would mean he actually wanted her.

It wouldn't just be getting up in front of a group of strangers who were judging her and insulting her if they didn't like what she did. Heck, the man would know she was a virgin. He wouldn't be expecting her to be good at it. And if she got upset, well...

A guy who's willing to pay to pop your cherry won't mind a bit of crying.

Emily bit her lower lip as she checked her emails. Nothing back from any of the applications she'd put in. No missed calls.

At the very least, she could apply to the site. She could always back out if she changed her mind, but if she didn't get her application in today, she would be too late.

Don't think about it too hard. Just treat it like another job application.

It kind of was, too. Since she was applying as a virgin, other than checking off that she had no sexual history, the website wanted her name and the same information that regular jobs required. She also needed to upload a clean bill of health—thankfully, she had that. She'd been able to go to a free clinic a few weeks ago, and she still had the paperwork.

At the time, she hadn't been sure it had been worth not picking up the extra shift that had come up for grabs, but she hadn't been to the doctor since before her mom had gone to jail and her dad dipped out, so she'd gone and waited all day in line to be seen. Then she'd gone to the library, scanned it, and sent it to her email. Now, she was so glad she had.

Next, she got to the section asking for pictures. She'd seen the kinds of pictures on the site, but thankfully, the other ones in the virgin section were a little less revealing. She supposed it was because they were going for the innocence angle. That helped her out.

Getting to her feet, she walked on unsteady legs to the bathroom, telling herself that she was unsteady from sitting for so long, not because she was freaking out. Nope, she was definitely not freaking out at all.

Thankfully, the bathroom was empty. Emily locked the door behind her and stood there in the harsh light, staring into the mirror. She looked...

haunted. Her eyes were too big, and her skin was a lot paler than normal, and when she tried to smile, it looked incredibly fake.

Good thing she didn't have to show her face.

Holding the camera at different angles, she took a bunch of pictures, careful to turn her face away from them. Tugging down the front of her shirt, she daringly got a shot of her ample cleavage.

None of it looked quite right. Maybe it was the lighting or her phone's crappy camera, but it didn't look the way she wanted it to. She felt stupid when she flipped through them, but she also didn't think she could do much better, so she uploaded them.

Even fifty thousand dollars would make a huge difference to her life.

What if no one bids on me?

Well, at least she'd be no worse off than before. Her pride and self-confidence might take a beating, but she didn't exactly have an abundance of those.

Taking a deep breath, she hit submit. It felt like something monumental should happen at that moment, but nothing did. There was no outcry, the power didn't flicker, and no one screamed at her that she was a whore... the world just kept going on around her.

Unlocking the door, she walked out. Not a single person looked her way.

She supposed it didn't really count as a life-changing event until it actually happened. All she'd done was send in an application to change her life. Heck, she didn't know if she'd actually even be approved.

She still didn't know if she wanted to be.

THE AUCTION SITE

DAMIAN

"**W**hat's that?"

Normally, Damian didn't butt into what his workers were doing, especially at the end of the day when they were technically off and just waiting for their ride, but he'd walked behind the row of seats in the waiting room where Paul was sitting and happened to glance over his shoulder. For one brief moment, he'd thought he'd seen Emily on the screen.

Looking up, Paul looked a bit guilty, but he shrugged. In his late twenties, he'd been working for Damian for about five years, so they'd gotten to know each other pretty well.

"It's an auction site for fulfilling your fantasies,

run by BDE," he said, his cheeks reddening a bit. That was the other way they'd gotten to know each other; Damian had found out Paul was kinky and sent him to a local munch. From there, he'd gone on to become a member at BDE. "It's all legit. I have a buddy who bought a fantasy off it last month."

"What?" Damian frowned. Braden hadn't mentioned anything like that to him. On the other hand, Braden often didn't go into detail about the day-to-day operations of the kink club because he knew both Damian and Desmond preferred to be kept out of it. They might technically be partners, but it was Braden's baby.

"See?" Paul angled the screen so Damian could lean over the back of his chair and see, flipping back to the home page, so he didn't get more than a glimpse of the woman who had caught his eye.

"Buy Your Fantasy... huh." Was the club hurting for money? No. Braden would have definitely told him about that. This was probably just some kind of new money-making venture. As Paul scrolled down the page, Damian recognized several BDE members in the pictures. It looked as if the next auction was coming up on Friday, and there were plenty of people selling... he wondered how many were buying. "What was that page you were looking at before?"

The woman who'd reminded him of Emily, even though he'd only been able to see her hair and body.

"Oh, that's the virgin auction. There are only a couple of options, and a new one just popped up." Paul clicked back. There she was.

It couldn't be Emily, of course. She didn't know anything about the club, and she would never do something like this. Besides, he was pretty sure she wasn't a virgin—she'd had a pretty serious boyfriend for a while before everything went to hell with her parents. While he'd tried to stay out of his daughter's business, when she'd decided she was ready, she'd asked him to take her to the doctor to get birth control. Friends tended to do things at the same time.

Besides, Emily was almost twenty-five now. There was no way she was still a virgin. Sure, she'd never brought anyone home to the trailer park that he knew of, but she was gone a lot, too. There was every chance she was spending time at some guy's place. And with Katrina across the country, Damian didn't get to keep up with Emily's life the way he had when Katrina had been home.

This young woman must be even younger, which made him feel even dirtier for the thought that was rising in his head. She *did* look a lot like Emily.

Similar body and curves. Similar hair. He couldn't see her face, but that only fueled his fantasy.

Fuck.

He could not be thinking what he was thinking.

"The virgins go for a lot," Paul said. "Especially because there's not many of them. Everything is pretty local, though. They've gotta be within a hundred miles of BDE to even sign up or be willing to travel nearby to fulfill their promise. I think that's why there are so many members on here. It's just a fun, harmless way of adding a little extra kick to your kink, ya know?"

"Sure." Damian had already made note of the website's name. He'd check it out more when he got home.

"Um, if you're interested, you'll need the password." It was as if Paul had read his mind. "They don't want just anyone getting on, you know. You've gotta be vetted and sign up for your own account to even look, and you need a password to even do that."

That made sense. It sounded like Braden was taking safety seriously, which was what he would expect. He was still surprised Braden hadn't mentioned it to him... but then, if it had only been running for a few months, he could see Braden deciding to wait until the next business meeting so he could give Damian and Desmond the rundown.

Sometimes, it was better to ask forgiveness than permission, especially because Desmond could be such a tight-ass.

"Can you give me the password?" he asked, amused by Paul's cagey reaction. Poor guy was acting like Damian had caught him watching porn at work. Well, maybe this kind of website wasn't much better, but he was off the clock and Damian wasn't going to give him a hard time about what he did on his own time.

"Oh, right. Yeah, sure, of course." Paul, like most of the members, knew Damian's brother ran BDE, but he probably didn't know that Damian was a partner, so he didn't seem to find the request odd.

Password in hand on the appointment card he grabbed off the front desk to write it down on, Damian headed home. He was going to peruse the site tonight and—maybe—think about the woman auctioning off her virginity.

It wasn't the virgin part that appealed to him so much as the fantasy... he could pretend she was Emily and that he was taking Emily's virginity. Which made him feel all kinds of a dirty pervert, but since it wouldn't actually be Emily...

Plus, if the young woman was putting herself up for auction, it probably meant she really needed the money. He could help her out and fulfill a fantasy of being with Emily, then maybe he'd be able to really focus on finding someone else without being distracted by Emily's existence. It wasn't just Emily's age that was the problem. It was also her relationship with his daughter, his former relationship with her dad, and not wanting to break her mom's trust.

Walking up into his trailer, he glanced up when the bus pulled up, not actually expecting to see anyone, then blinked in surprise when he saw Emily get off. For a moment, he thought he was imagining her just because she was on his mind, but no, there she was.

Huh.

Her work schedule must have changed. Or maybe she just needed a night off.

When she looked up, he raised his hand in greeting before turning away to open his door. Even though she couldn't possibly know what he was thinking, he felt vulnerable, as if somehow she'd see something or get a hint of his thoughts if she looked hard enough. Or maybe it was just guilt turning him around because he knew that what he was fantasizing about—what he wanted—was wrong.

Fuck, he needed to get her out of his head.

The auction might be his best chance.

Then he could keep his promise to Anita to find a

real date, someone he could have an actual relation-ship with.

EMILY

Waving back at Katrina's hot dad, Emily sighed when he turned around so fast, she was pretty sure he hadn't actually seen her wave. She'd had such a crush on him in high school, even though she knew he'd never look at her that way. More than once, she'd teased Katrina about how hot he was while her bestie overdramatically gagged and pretended to throw up.

He was the park DILF, and there was no way around that.

He'd been really great when she was growing up. She hadn't noticed him *that way* until she'd started noticing boys in general. Even then, all of her admiration happened from afar. Especially since he'd been her dad's best friend. Then, slowly, her dad had started saying more and more awful things about her mom, her, Katrina... He'd stopped watching the news and only watched the internet, claiming no one was telling the truth. Then he'd started blaming women and anyone who wasn't white for bringing him down.

Eventually, after he said something really nasty

about black people in front of Katrina, Mr. Elliott stopped letting Katrina go to Emily's trailer. She'd had to go to Katrina's, which she hadn't minded. Katrina's was nicer at that point, and Mr. Elliott always kept it clean... plus, her father's temper had started to become more unpredictable, and her mom had started checking out.

After it all came to a head, Mr. Elliott kind of disappeared from her life. Katrina had already left for college, and there was no real reason for her to see him, but she missed having his presence in her life. It also didn't help her crush since all she had left was fantasies, and they started taking a decidedly wicked turn.

Something he would have been horrified to know, especially since he'd pulled away. Clearly, the only reason he'd been a part of her life had been her dad and Katrina, and when his friendship with her dad ended and Katrina moved, that had been that.

He was still really freaking hot.

If someone like him bought her virginity, that wouldn't be so bad at all.

Keeping her head down as her face heated with a hot blush, she trudged down the street to her trailer, waving to several of her neighbors as she passed. Unlike Mr. Elliott, they actually saw her.

"You're home early," called Mrs. Martine, who was

out watering her flowers. The older woman often kept an eye out for Emily on her way home, for which she was grateful. Everyone knew everyone in the park, but that didn't mean everyone was very neighborly. Mrs. Martine was, though, and she knew Emily's work schedule like it was her own.

Emily hesitated but decided she wasn't ready to talk about her job situation yet. Not until she either had a new one or didn't need one anymore. But she could fudge it a little bit. Maybe ease her neighbor into the change.

"The owner's niece needs a job, so she's taking some shifts," she replied, temporizing the truth rather than outright lying.

"Oh, well, a night off for you. Isn't that nice?" Mrs. Martine smiled, and Emily pushed the edges of her lips to curve as well.

"Yes." Now, that was an outright lie. She would much rather be at work earning money than at home fretting over her lack of a job and freaking out about the fact her application to auction off her virginity had been accepted not even ten minutes after she'd uploaded it.

Giving Mrs. Martine another wave, Emily went into her trailer. Her stomach grumbled since she hadn't had anything to eat all day. Thank goodness for the food she'd been sent home with from the restaurant. She had to make it last, but it was something. Maybe tomorrow, she'd eat a roll or something for breakfast, so she wasn't quite so hungry at the end of the day. She was already missing the staff meals at the diner.

With every bite, she chewed as slowly as she could, savoring the flavors. She even had a little bit of fruit left for dessert, so the day wasn't so bad.

All she had to do was prep herself for the reality of popping her cherry in order to fix her life. It couldn't be that hard, right? All she had to do was lie there. Her buyer wouldn't expect her to know what she was doing. He wouldn't want her to—that was the point.

Emily chewed on her spoon as she stared at the stain on the wall where her dad had thrown a pot of spaghetti sauce all those years ago.

What if the guy she got was violent? Or cruel? What if he was wildly unattractive?

He's not going to be Prince Charming. Might as well get that through your head right away, dummy.

It wasn't about the guy.

It just wasn't.

It was about changing her life. It was about financial security. It was about keeping her power on, not getting kicked out of her parents' trailer, and having enough food to eat. It was about never having to admit to her mom or Katrina how bad things had gotten.

If she got enough money, maybe she could even take some classes at the community college or travel to one of the trade schools. Maybe be able to afford the commute to one of the areas with nicer restaurants and start working at one of those.

Right now, she didn't have to face reality, so she stared at the wall and dreamed.

❧ 6 ❧

COUNTING DOWN THE DAYS

DAMIAN

Despite his distraction wondering why Emily was home tonight instead of working—and somehow feeling dirtier for looking at her doppelganger on the auction website while she was only a few blocks away from him rather than at work—Damian booted up his computer and pulled up the site. The password worked just like Paul said it would, sending him to an application for the auction site. Since he was a BDE member, he didn't actually have to provide much. His membership number and password to *that* site got him in easily.

From there, all he had to do was set up how he was going to pay and get approved for how high he could bid. Clearly, Braden had thought ahead to make sure he didn't need to worry about anyone bidding amounts they couldn't afford.

Despite feeling like a perv, the first page Damian went to after that was the virgin auction to stare at the Emily look-alike.

Curvy, like her, long light brown hair, like her. It wasn't like Emily's hair color was uncommon. Her username was "Sunshine." After taking a long look at the pictures, unsure of whether or not he was happy he couldn't see the young woman's face, he decided to check out the rest of the site. Maybe someone else would catch his eye. Or maybe he would find someone who also resembled Emily, who he could bid on who wasn't a young virgin.

There were a few with some similarities. The long, light brown hair. The curves. But none that resembled her as much as Sunshine.

The more he thought about it, the more he hated the idea of Sunshine getting someone who wouldn't appreciate her. Yes, there were a couple other virgins on the site, but it wasn't as though he could buy all of them. And, if he was being truthful, he didn't want to.

There was only one who called to him, only one he could even imagine bidding on. The one that looked like the girl he couldn't have.

He couldn't have Emily, but he could bid on

Sunshine. Give her a good night, a great night even. Ensure the loss of her virginity gave her the money she must need *and* that she received pleasure from it. Then he could hopefully move on with his life and find someone age-appropriate, having purged the fantasy from his system.

No, she wasn't Emily, but he could make it close enough.

His phone ringing made him jump guiltily, and he slammed the laptop shut so he wasn't looking at the site anymore. There was no way he could have that up and visible while he answered his daughter's phone call.

"Hey, honey." He cleared his throat, realizing he sounded a little odd. Thankfully, she didn't seem to notice.

"Hey, Dad. I just wanted to call to let you know I got into a show here!"

"What? I didn't even know you were auditioning for anything." He couldn't help but smile. Even though she was serious about her studies, Katrina had always had a theatrical bent. He wanted to ask if she thought that being in a show might affect her studies, but he knew she wouldn't have auditioned if she was worried about that. She was an adult now, and he needed to try to trust her to take care of her own schedule.

Plus, if he nagged her too much, she might stop calling him with news.

"Well, I didn't want to tell you in case I didn't get it, but I'm going to be in the Vagina Monologues in June!"

"Great?" It came out as more of a question than a congratulation.

Katrina's laugh echoed over the phone. "It's a bunch of monologues by women about their vaginas. You're going to come see me in it, right?" she asked, sounding perfectly gleeful.

"Yup, of course, sweetie. So proud of you." He rubbed his forehead. "Do I want to ask what part you have?" She wasn't doing this to torture him. Probably. No, that would just be a happy byproduct for her.

"They haven't been assigned yet. A group of us got in, and during our first rehearsal, we'll go through them, and they'll be assigned to us. Everyone's going to do at least two, and a few people might get to do three." She was clearly excited.

"That's great, honey." He did his best to drum up some sincere enthusiasm. "I hope you get whatever it is you want to do."

Katrina snickered.

She was having a little too much fun at his expense, but he wasn't going to complain. Part of him wanted to ask if she'd called Emily the night before, but—still feeling guilty about the website that would reappear as soon as he opened his laptop back up—he couldn't bring himself to bring her up. Besides, he really didn't need to hear his daughter call him Trailer Park Daddy again, especially not right after talking about vagina monologues.

She told him a bit about how they'd become a show, reassured him it wouldn't interfere with her studies—though he didn't ask—and said that she would wait to get a part-time job until after the show was over. None of which he asked about, but she clearly knew he'd be concerned.

Damn, he'd gotten lucky with what a good kid she was.

"Are you making dinner?" she asked when she heard him moving pots and pans around.

"Yeah."

"Oh, okay, then I'll let you go."

"I can keep talking." Honestly, he'd be happy to stay on the phone with her all night. When she was on the phone with him, he knew she was okay.

It was damn hard being a long-distance dad.

"No, I've got some things to do this afternoon. I'll call you as soon as I know which vaginas I get," she teased.

Damian groaned. "You do that. Love you, sweetie."

"Love you, Dad. Talk to you later. Bye!"

"Good night." Sighing heavily, he ended the call and set his phone down so he could work on getting dinner ready. But he couldn't stop glancing over at the computer every now and then, knowing what he would see as soon as he opened it again.

Even though he silently said he was still deciding, deep down, he already knew what he was going to do.

EMILY

Every morning, Emily went out looking for a new job. Every evening, she came back with nothing to show for it. She stopped by the diner, but unfortunately, it seemed like Marianne's nieces were working out just fine. The cook on duty did sneak her another staff meal, which she nearly broke down and cried over, just because she was so grateful.

That one little drop of kindness meant the world to her.

She was currently avoiding Katrina's calls, though they'd texted back and forth a few times.

In the evenings, Emily looked at the numbers. What she could do with an extra ten thousand dollars. An extra twenty thousand. An extra fifty thousand. She didn't dare dream bigger than that, at least not on paper. It was too big, too scary to think that might be possible.

No matter how she added it up, it was always worth it. Ten thousand dollars would change her whole life.

Her stomach ached with hunger every day, but she was too worried about what would happen next week if she ate all her food this week. Dumpster diving hadn't turned out very well, though she had found some stale donuts in a plastic bag and taken those home with her to freeze as well. Though if she ended up getting kicked out of the trailer, she wasn't sure that all the food she was freezing was going to end up doing her any good.

She'd been maintaining a delicate balance of paying for things so that nothing got turned off and nothing was ever more than two months behind, but she was on her third month of not paying the power bill, and next month, the trailer park would need to be paid, or she could be evicted.

Friday afternoon, she splurged on a bus ticket and went to visit her mom. She needed to see her.

Thankfully, the jail her mom was in was close to the town and wasn't high-security. Emily signed in and went to the visiting area, smiling what felt like her first genuine smile of the week when her mom appeared and sat down across from her. She looked good. Better than she had when she'd gone into the jail and had been strung out most of the time.

Her cheeks had filled out, as had her curvy frame, which she'd lost when she'd been doing drugs. Now, she filled out her jumpsuit, and the hair that was pulled back into a ponytail was glossy and healthy-looking. Just seeing her like this eased something in Emily's heart.

Granted, she wished she was seeing her mom outside of the jail, but at least her mom had been able to get help and was doing so much better.

"Hey, baby." Her mom opened her arms wide as Emily got to her feet.

It was impossible to forget where they were when there were several other visits happening at nearby tables and guards at both doors, but when she closed her eyes, Emily could almost pretend they were back at the trailer, her mom hugging her the way she had when Emily was a child. Tears sprang to her eyes, and she quickly blinked them away.

"Hey, Mom," she said as they parted and moved to their seats on opposite sides of the table.

"Thanks for coming to visit me. I feel like it's been forever." Her mom smiled at her, taking some of the sting out of the words. Emily knew her mom wasn't trying to guilt-trip her, but she felt it, anyway.

"I've been busy at work."

"You are a hard worker. I hope you're taking some time to have fun, too?" It was the same conversation they had every time Emily came to visit.

She pushed her usual smile onto her lips. "Sure. You know, it's harder with Katrina gone." She shrugged. "I spent a lot of time at the library this week."

"You and your books." Her mom grinned. "Read anything good?"

"Actually, I was mostly using their internet. I think it's time for me to find a new job." She'd lost the previous one, but it sounded better this way, and she got to watch her mother's eyes light up with approval rather than cloud with disappointment or guilt over being stuck in jail when her daughter needed her help.

"Oh, that would be great! Do you know what you want to do?"

She loved that her mom just assumed she could do anything. Well, she loved and hated it. Loved her mom's belief in her. Hated that she was bound to disappoint her. Though if she got enough money from selling her virginity, maybe she could go to some kind of trade school or college and get the kind of job that would make her mother proud.

It wasn't like she needed her master's like Katrina. Just... something.

"I don't really know. Something that doesn't involve working doubles for tips." Especially for very small tips, which were all she'd gotten at the diner. "Maybe something where I can work my way up. I always thought I'd make a good locksmith."

Unfortunately, the locksmith wasn't currently taking on anyone new, but it was still a fun thought, and it made her mom laugh.

"I always thought you would end up doing something with numbers. Maybe become an accountant," her mom said dreamily.

That was one of the options Emily had looked at if she got fifty thousand dollars. She'd be able to afford some schooling, then get a job working somewhere until she got her CPA. Accounting was a good, solid, stable career. And she'd always been good with numbers.

She liked numbers. Numbers were safe and secure, and they always came back with the same result as long as the equation was done correctly. There were no surprises with numbers. Of course, she hadn't liked numbers as much when she'd started having to use them to figure out how she was going to live on not-enough money, but she'd been lucky she was so good at them. She'd made it this far.

Seeing how proud and happy her mom was of her, Emily vowed that by the time her mom got out of jail, she would make sure her mom had a trailer to come home to, one with the power on and the bills paid up. If she needed reassurance she was making the right decision, she was getting it now.

7

THE AUCTION

EMILY

Oh fuck, oh fuck, oh fuck...

What was I thinking?

The surety that she'd felt at the jail had faded by the time the bus dropped Emily off in front of the trailer park.

It was all well and good to think about the future and what she would be able to do with money and what she wanted for her mom, but the auction was starting in two hours, and the reality of what she had to do to get that future was hitting home. On the way home, she'd stupidly checked her email and seen the confirmation message that she was live, and the bidding would be starting soon, and she'd immediately felt nauseous.

All the confidence she'd had melted away in the harsh face of the truth.

She was selling her body.

Selling her virginity.

Because she needed the money.

It was horrific, degrading, and... necessary. Or at least the best path she could see out of her current situation, which had become more dire than she'd wanted to admit. Which was how she'd found herself here.

Anxiety frazzled her, riding her as she headed to her trailer, waving at the neighbors she passed. Mrs. Martine wasn't outside, so at least no one stopped her to talk. She wasn't sure she would be able to converse without falling apart and admitting what was happening.

Once safely inside, she went on autopilot, putting together a small meal to eat. For the first time in days, her stomach wasn't growling. It was too tied in knots. She didn't feel any hunger. All she felt was her nervousness. She had to force herself to take bites and chew them because she knew she needed to eat something.

She just hoped she didn't throw it up later when someone had bought her virginity.

If someone bought her virginity.

God, she didn't know which outcome would be worse.

Done with her meal, she started manically cleaning, constantly looking at the clock. The time until the auction started was dragging on.

She could still back out. She didn't have to do this. Maybe she could find another way. Having sex for the first time with a complete stranger for money... that wasn't her. She was a good girl. She'd gotten good grades. She'd tried to do everything right her whole life, and this was where it had gotten her?

Tears started welling up, and she shook her head angrily, looking up at the clock again.

At that exact moment, the power in the trailer died.

Emily froze in place... but only for a moment.

She darted over to the window, but she knew what she was going to see before she got there because she could see the lights even before she looked outside. Everyone else's lights were still on. It was only her power that had just been turned off.

Closing her eyes, she mentally went over her payment schedule, and her heart sank. She'd been so distracted, she'd forgotten the power was due now. No, she hadn't forgotten. She'd pushed it out of her mind because there hadn't been anything she could do about it. She'd known having it turned off was a possibility, but there had been a tiny part of her that hoped if she ignored it, nothing would happen.

She was out of options.

Sinking down to the floor, Emily pulled her knees to her chest and felt the first sob heave out of her. She couldn't stop it.

It was like a dam bursting. Once the first tear fell, she couldn't push any others back. She rocked on the stained linoleum, holding herself because there was no one there to hold her, wishing she could feel her mother's arms around her again. Wishing there was someone there to tell her that everything would be okay.

She wished for a fairy godmother, for other impossible things, for someone to come bursting through the door to save her. She'd always believed in self-rescuing princesses, believed she could figure things out for herself, but if a white knight came to sweep her off her feet right now, she would cling to him and thank him and cry tears of joy.

Heck, in a fucked-up way, wasn't that what she was doing?

Except it wouldn't be a white knight—it would be a strange man who was willing to pay to take some-one's virginity.

But the money would rescue her.

Since she was the one putting herself up for the

auction, could she consider that the act of a self-rescuing princess?

The laugh that puffed out of her finally broke the stranglehold her tears had on her. A self-rescuing princess selling her virginity to get her happily ever after—prince not included.

What a sad fucking fairy tale.

But that was reality, wasn't it? There were no truly happy endings, but she could have a happier ending than she was going to get if she never did anything to change her situation. She would have the money to make her life better.

So, fuck the prince and fuck the white knight and fuck Ron and fuck her dad and fuck everything.

Emily was going to do what needed to be done.

If that meant selling her virginity, then so be it.

Sniffling again, she got to her feet, brushed herself off, and picked up her phone to turn it off. She glanced at the time before she did so. The auction was starting, but without power, she couldn't charge her phone. Despite the temptation to sit and watch, it was better to turn it off so she could check it in the morning and see the final result.

This was the last-ditch effort. Tomorrow morning, she would wake up either a woman about to become financially secure or a woman who was going to lose everything. Now that the power was out, everything else was going to tumble down like a stack of cards, especially with no new job.

She needed the money.

Turning off her phone, she headed to her room and laid down on the lumpy mattress, tugging the sheets over her head. She didn't think she would fall asleep quickly, but she was so exhausted that once she put her head down, the blissful darkness came up to claim her almost immediately.

DAMIAN

Was he really going to go through with this?

One minute until the auction began.

It would run for three hours.

I don't know if I can go through with this.

Unfortunately, his obsession with Emily seemed to have been replaced by Sunshine ever since he'd realized she was *available*. The idea of giving her a good night, of helping her, had lodged in his brain and didn't want to let go.

On the upside, he hadn't thought about Emily that way in days.

On the downside, he wasn't sure that made him any better.

Sunshine was still too young for him, but she wasn't his daughter's best friend. Was too young really that big a deal? This way, he could ensure her first time was a good experience. That it was pleasurable. Memorable for reasons other than she was selling it.

Maybe he was assigning motivations where there were none. Maybe she was like the others on the site, selling something because she had a fantasy. Maybe she wasn't even a virgin.

That's it. Keep justifying it in your head because you know what you want to do.

Fuck.

When was the last time he'd done something for himself?

He couldn't remember. So, maybe it was high past time.

Yet, when he signed onto the site, he still couldn't bring himself to put in an immediate bid.

It wasn't stopping anyone else.

He scrolled through, just to see, but the virgin auction was definitely racking up the bids the fastest, and Sunshine was the second-most-popular item. Bids were already close to a hundred thousand dollars.

Why did I bother moving all that money around this week if I'm not going to use it?

He'd prepared for this, anticipating the bidding

could get crazy and wanting to be prepared, just in case. Normally, he didn't spend a lot of money. He kept it in various investments and savings—not just his shops and the club, but scattered around. He'd gathered a hefty chunk together over the past few days, specifically so he could bid on Sunshine.

So, do it. Or are you going to let another opportunity to actually have something you want pass you by?

That's what he'd been doing because it had been easier. Letting life pass him by. Focusing on Katrina. Now, he wanted something for himself, and he was hesitating.

It's not as simple as something for yourself when it affects someone else.

Right, but in a good way.

For whatever reason, Sunshine wanted money. Damian had money. And he could finally purge Emily from his head. Sunshine had already replaced her, but she was a figment, a fantasy. When the night was over, he'd be able to move on with his life.

Ideally, without his preoccupation with his daughter's best friend.

Even so, it wasn't until the last half hour of the auction that he joined in the bidding, which had slowed considerably after it hit two hundred thousand dollars. It looked like it was down to two bidders when Damian entered his first bid. Heat flushed through him as he stared at the little marker that let him know he currently had the highest bid.

A minute passed.

Two.

Five.

Was that it? One bid and... no.

Another bid came through from one of the two bidders left.

Damian waited to see if the other previous bidder would put in another bid. It took about ten minutes, but he did.

Making himself wait a few minutes, Damian added another.

After about five minutes, the first bidder outbid him again.

There were only ten minutes left in the auction.

Damian upped the bid again. Two hundred forty thousand dollars.

The last time he'd spent that much money, he'd bought an entire shop. Made an investment in his future, something he could leave to his daughter and use to provide for her in the meantime.

What the fuck am I doing?

Yet he already knew he wasn't going to walk away.

He felt hot. Nervous.

But he couldn't bring himself to close down the laptop and go. Not now that he was in it. He was determined to be the highest bidder. He'd already gotten this far. He'd started bidding; he was going to finish it.

It was possible he could be a little overly competitive because he knew at least part of his reasoning was just wanting to win. But part of it was because he'd been watching the other two bidders, and who knew what their motivations were? The only person whose motivations he could be sure of were his own.

What if he didn't win and Sunshine got hurt? Or ended up with a cold, callous winning bidder who just wanted to say he'd slept with a virgin? What if she had a terrible night because she got stuck with an asshole who didn't care about making it a good experience for her?

Sure, the other guy might be just like Damian, with plans to make it good for her, but he might not. There was no way for Damian to know.

In the last few minutes, the bidding became more and more fierce, a thousand dollars at a time, until it was over two hundred and sixty thousand.

Something flashed red on his screen, and his heart sank, thinking he'd lost, but then his eyes adjusted, and he realized it was asking for his final bid. There was a countdown clock for the final minute and also the warning that whatever he bid, he needed to outbid his opponent to win, without being able to see what they were bidding.

What was this, Jeopardy rules?

Fuck.

Three hundred thousand dollars. If the other guy bid more, it just wasn't meant to be, and he'd tried his best.

Damian put in the bid and sat back and watched the red numbers roll by until they reached zero, and the screen flashed back to Sunshine's auction page.

The top of the page had changed.

Winning Bid placed by TrailerParkDaddy.

Relief flooded through his chest as he breathed out a sigh of air he hadn't known he was holding.

He won.

8

THE CONTRACT

EMILY

She woke with a start, coming awake all of a sudden and all at once, but without knowing why. There was no loud knock, no sound, no abrupt change in light that woke her.

It took her a moment to remember why she was so on edge, then she scrambled for her phone, turning it on. While she was waiting, she stared morosely at her dark lamp. The power was still gone. Not that she'd really thought it was an accident. If she actually opened the last bill they'd sent her—the one with the intimidating red *FINAL NOTICE* printed on the outside—she was sure she'd see the warning that it was going to be turned off if she didn't pay soon.

She giggled somewhat hysterically and pulled the mac and cheese from her freezer. Without electricity, there was no point in hoarding it anymore.

The problem was she didn't bother to open them because when she'd had her payments planned out, it never got to that point. So, she hadn't known what day it was going to happen. She'd only known it was soon.

Her phone chimed. Battery at fifty percent. Not too bad. She could go back to the library today to charge it. She'd have to.

Pulling up her email, she could feel the anxiety sliding around her stomach. It didn't feel like butter-flies, more like eels writhing inside her.

Auction Contract and Details Inside

The third email's subject, the only email that wasn't spam mail trying to sell her something, stared back at her from her phone screen. The eels in her stomach writhed again, thrashing about and making her gorge rise. But she opened the email.

And almost threw up immediately.

Three hundred thousand dollars.

Three hundred thousand dollars?

It was a trick. It had to be.

She pressed a hand to her stomach, trying not to heave.

Three hundred thousand dollars?

She blinked and refocused.

Legal jargon explained that of the three-hundred-thousand-dollar winning bid on her virginity, she would receive two hundred and twenty-five thousand dollars. If she hadn't already been sitting on her bed, she would have collapsed.

Two hundred and twenty-five thousand dollars?

It was still an impossible amount.

Leaning over, she put her head between her knees, taking deep breaths as the panic inside her whirled. She didn't even know why she was panicking. This was beyond the answer to her prayers, far beyond what she had hoped for, yet she was freaking out even more than if it had been ten thousand dollars.

More than two hundred thousand dollars!

The trailer she lived in wasn't even worth that much.

Emily gulped.

That really was life-changing money.

I could get a car. I could move. I could go to school. I could...

Her thoughts were racing, chaotic, but she pushed that all away. First, she had to get the money. Since her breathing had evened out, she lifted her head and kept reading the email.

There were directions in it passed on from her

buyer. All communications between them would be handled via the auction site, for safety, which was a relief. She didn't have to set up anything on her own. The money was currently verified and waiting in escrow, and once she and the buyer signed off on the task being completed, the money would be transferred to her bank account. The site did not handle taxes. Emily made a mental note to make sure to look into what she would need to do for that, but even that little mental note felt very far away, as if it belonged to someone else.

She'd never needed to do anything like that before.

Putting down the phone, she pinched herself. Just in case. Not that she'd ever tried to pinch herself in a dream in case she was dreaming, so just the attempt told her something, but...

Ow.

Definitely awake.

Awake and soon to be losing her virginity but gaining everything she needed to actually *live.*

Her phone chimed with another incoming email from the site. Still feeling like everything was surreal, Emily opened it to see what the follow-up was.

It was a message from her buyer, passed on through the website. If she'd realized, she probably wouldn't have opened it—she would have been too terrified. So, it was a good thing she hadn't known… because the message was kind of nice.

Hello, Sunshine,

You can call me Master D. I wanted to reassure you that I'm going to take care of you for your first time. I want it to be as good for you as it can possibly be.

In that vein, at the bottom of this email, I have included a link to a gift card so you can buy yourself something to wear for the evening. I particularly like silk and lace, but I want you to have whatever you desire. My main request is that you also purchase a mask. I will be wearing one as well. I would like to keep this pure fantasy and also preserve our identities should we ever run across each other out in the world. Let me know if this meets with your approval, or we can discuss other options.

I am free both nights this weekend or the next. If a week-night would work better for you, I can arrange that as well.

Let me know when will be best for you and if there's a particular location that is preferable. If you'd like to meet at Club BDE, we can, or at a hotel if that's your preference. Once I have your answer for time and town, I will make the arrangements.

Looking forward to meeting you,
Master D

Holy...

Emily felt a little weak in the knees again. The man was either full of charisma and a total smooth talker, or he was an absolute snake in the grass. Then her jaw dropped when she saw the attached gift certificate.

A thousand dollars? To buy sexy underwear and a mask?

She couldn't remember the last time she'd bought underwear in anything but a pack. She got her bras from the local thrift store, then she wore them out to holey messes before replacing them.

A thousand dollars?

She didn't even know where to go to spend that kind of money on underwear. Then again, she didn't know where to go to spend any kind of money on sexy underwear. It might have been easier if it was for a specific store, but she could go *anywhere.*

No, that was too scary. Besides, she didn't have a car.

Online. There had to be something she could find online. Maybe get it overnight shipped? She had the money for it. She couldn't tell Master D what day she could see him until she was sure she would have what he requested of her. And she was really grateful he was interested in anonymity even though she wasn't sure she'd be able to call him Master D with a straight face.

She needed to see him as soon as possible. She needed her power back on. She needed... she needed to start her life over.

That's what that kind of money was. A reset.

As much as she wanted to sit down and start budgeting things out—because she knew how easy it would be to blow through that kind of money if she didn't plan carefully; there was a reason lottery winners often went broke—she started looking for underwear instead. A thousand dollars...

Her stomach grumbled.

There were so many things she could use a thousand dollars for. Would it be unethical to order some other things she needed rather than use it all for one silk nightie and a mask? Because she was finding what looked like some really nice ones, all for less than a hundred.

In the end, her total came to less than four hundred dollars, and even that made her blanch because she had never spent that much money on clothing before. She got a silk gown and matching thong, a mask, and a pair of cute kitten-heel shoes, all with overnight shipping. The fact that it added up to nearly four hundred dollars made her almost nauseous that she was spending that much on so little.

At least she could write Master D back. She would ask for tomorrow night. That left her only one night with no power. Hopefully, no one would notice that her trailer had gone dark. Mrs. Martine was very kind, but she was also a bit of a gossip. Emily didn't want everyone to know how bad things had gotten right before she managed to fix everything.

Especially since she didn't want anyone asking *how* she fixed everything.

DAMIAN

Hello Master D,

Thank you so much for your generosity. I have ordered a silk gown as you requested, along with everything I need to go with it, including the mask. I appreciate the offer of anonymity and would like that as well. This is very strange for me, but I appreciate everything you are doing to help me be comfortable.

Would Sunday night, tomorrow night, be acceptable? If I can use your gift card, I can get a ride to a hotel. There was more than enough left over, if you don't mind me using it for that. And I can return everything I didn't use on the gift card to you.

Please let me know where and when you would like to meet.

Thank you so much again,
Sunshine

Shaking his head, Damian couldn't decide if he was charmed or worried. Sunshine seemed naïve. He couldn't help but shake his head at the idea that, after paying three hundred thousand dollars for her virginity, he would be worried about a thousand-dollar gift card.

Before he replied, though, he made a reservation and contacted the site to see if he could send a car to pick her up. Considering she was trying to return the remainder of a gift card, he wanted to make sure she was taken care of. It only took a few minutes for confirmation to come through—whatever he wanted to do, the auction house would take care of it, so she could keep her address safe, and he could ensure she got what she needed.

It didn't take him long to get everything set up and email her back with instructions. Sunday night...

tomorrow night. Fuck. He felt that little bit of guilty regret again... but hell. It was consensual.

Besides, with it being done out of BDE, he trusted that Braden had found some way to make sure it was legal. After all, their other brother Desmond was a former cop and had a constant stick up his ass when it came to following the law. It was part of the reason he and Damian had always butted heads—Desmond was a rule follower, and Damian only followed the rules he wanted to.

Braden did his best to be the peacemaker between them, which meant when something was this important—especially anything that affected the club Desmond was part owner of—he would make sure it was all on the up and up.

Once everything was set up, he emailed Sunshine back.

Hello, Sunshine,

Keep the gift certificate. It's for you, however you wish to use it.

Don't worry about a thing for tomorrow, just be ready to leave at 5 p.m., which is when the car will come pick you up. I've made arrangements through the auction site; they're handling the reservations and the directions for me, for your privacy, so you don't have to do anything.

You'll receive instructions tomorrow when you get in the car.

Take care,
Master D

There. That way, she knew she could spend the money, which was always what he'd intended. Perhaps she was just looking for extra money, and that's why she'd put herself up for auction, but perhaps she was in real need. Just in case it was the latter, he wanted her to be provided for.

Now, he just needed to make sure he had everything he needed for tomorrow night—a mask for himself, some tattoo concealer to cover up his most identifying marks, and a supply of condoms. At least one condom. The contract didn't cover more sex than the one time, he supposed, but a man could always hope.

If he made it good for her, she might be amenable to more.

Shrugging on his leather jacket, he grabbed his helmet and headed out to his bike. The Ducati wasn't the fanciest bike on the market, but it was the one he'd bought right after he and Anita had gotten married, and he hadn't been able to give it up. At this point, it didn't have many of its original parts, but that was okay. It still felt the same.

Before turning onto the main road through the park, he glanced to the left to make sure no one was coming and saw Emily trudging her way up the road. His dick twitched with interest, but he didn't have the same overpowering reaction of lust he normally did. His preoccupation with Sunshine was already working in his favor.

Even better, after looking so upset earlier this week, tonight she had a huge smile on her face. Good. Seemed like everyone was having a good weekend. And his was only going to get better from here.

9

PREPARING FOR MASTER D

EMILY

A freaking limo pulled up in front of the apartment building where Emily was waiting on the steps to be picked up. The chauffeur got out and peered up at her through squinted eyes.

"Emily Graham?" he asked.

Her heart nearly stopped in panic before rational thought reasserted itself. He knew her name because she'd had to put in her legal name to be put up for auction, so the site had her details, but that didn't mean Master D did. And the site had arranged for the pickup.

She'd requested it at the apartment building near the diner rather than the trailer park because she hadn't wanted any questions from her neighbors about why she was being picked up. She was triply glad she'd done so now. She'd been worried about Mrs. Martine or one of the others asking a bunch of questions about a normal car. If an actual stretch limo had shown up...

No one would have talked about anything else for days.

Already, she was getting some looks from people who were walking along the street. One little boy was pointing, tugging on his mom's arm, with wide eyes and his mouth open in shock. He'd probably never seen a limo before outside of a movie. Emily had ridden in one once, to prom, thanks to Mr. Elliott. Katrina had insisted that they be able to go together and hadn't been willing to take no for an answer. Emily had insisted on coming in and giving their trailer a deep clean in repayment, and Mr. Elliott had agreed to let her clean the common spaces, so she didn't feel so bad about it.

Still, that had been entirely different. That had been a whole group of them sharing the cost. This was just for her.

The chauffeur came up the steps with a cheerful smile. Picking up her bag, he winked at her.

"You are Ms. Graham, correct?" he asked.

"Yes... here..." She fumbled for her ID and

managed to hand it to him without dropping it. He was still holding her bag as he looked at it and gave a little nod.

"Great, come with me, ma'am."

Ma'am? Was she old enough to be a ma'am? She was pretty sure the chauffeur was older than her.

Feeling like she was back in the same crazy dream state she'd felt when she'd seen the auction results, she followed the chauffeur down to the car, where he opened the door to let her in.

"Please sit down, Ms. Graham. My name is Tim, and I'm here to take care of you. There's water and soda in the mini-fridge, the champagne is open and on ice. I believe you'll be having dinner at the hotel, but if you need anything to eat on the way, just let me know, and we can stop wherever you'd like." He grinned at her again, as though he was enjoying her reactions.

"Champagne?" Her voice squeaked. Even seeing the stretch limo, she hadn't expected anything more than just a ride.

"That's right. Have a seat and enjoy, ma'am."

"Please call me Emily," she said as she got into the car.

The seats were black leather, the interior as luxurious as any limo from a movie... and all for her. A very different experience than her prom night when she'd been crammed in with seven other teenagers, all of them vying for elbow room and giggling.

The door closed behind her, and she sank down onto the seat beside the champagne. She'd never had champagne before. Never really wanted to drink before, not after her dad... But if there was ever a time for a drink, it was now.

She was on her way to lose her virginity, after all. Liquid courage, that's what it was called. Not something she wanted to rely on, but in this one instance...

Besides, it was open. It would be rude not to partake when it had already been opened. She wouldn't get drunk, but maybe it would help take off some of the nerves.

Tim got into the front seat and glanced through the open partition.

"Let me know if you'd like some privacy, ma'am. There are some buttons to your right... yeah, that one right there, if you want to put the partition up, you can do it whenever you feel like. There's also an intercom once the window is up."

"Oh... thank you." Emily wasn't sure how she felt. Part of her wanted the partition up, so she could have some privacy to try to adjust to what was going on. Part of her wanted it down, so she could have some human contact and company, especially since Tim seemed nice.

She wondered if he knew what she was on her way to do.

Probably not.

Pouring herself a glass of champagne—well, more like a quarter of a glass because she somehow managed to pour mostly bubbles—Emily took a small sip. The bubbles were very bubbly, popping inside her mouth, and something about the drink made her tongue dry even though it was wet. The taste wasn't exactly what she'd expected. It wasn't fruity or anything, and it definitely didn't taste like grapes, but she didn't dislike it.

Watching the streets go by, and after a few more sips of champagne, she got up the courage to ask Tim a question.

"Are you allowed to tell me where we're going?"

"Oh, yes, ma'am, we're headed to the Ryder Manor."

Emily's jaw dropped.

As if the limo and the money he was paying her wasn't enough... she didn't know what she'd expected exactly. Not a seedy motel, probably, though somehow that would have felt more familiar, almost reassuring. But the Ryder? That was a wildly expensive extravagance for one night, especially after everything else he was already paying for. She didn't know anyone who had ever stayed there. The rooms went for a thousand dollars a night.

Which he already sent you for freaking lingerie, so why not for a hotel room?

She supposed that was what people with more money than they needed did.

She could understand the impulse. Yesterday, she'd used the remainder of the gift card to get her power back on, then to order groceries and a few other things online, splurging when she'd done it. She'd gotten the good cheese, fresh fruit, a carton of ice cream, name-brand shampoo and conditioner, two pairs of underwear that didn't come in a pack, and two new bras. She hadn't gone wild, of course. She was going to have to watch her spending even after she got the full amount from the auction because she needed it to go as far as possible.

After all, she still didn't have a new job.

But so many options were going to open up for her. She was going to get a car, nothing fancy, definitely used, but a good one that was in good condition. She was sure Mr. Elliott would look at it for her. She could use it to drive into Charleston for a better job. In the meantime, she could use the car to do deliveries or something, so she was still making some money. She'd heard people could do pretty well with delivery services, but without a car, she never considered it a possibility for herself.

A whole new world. All she had to do was have sex with a stranger.

She looked around the limo, Sasha's voice echoing in her head. It wasn't just the money that was making this special, though. Whoever Master D really was, he was living up to his promise to take care of her.

❧

DAMIAN

Sunshine was getting to the hotel at six, but Damian wouldn't get there until eight. The limo would take her to the Ryder, where she'd be greeted, shown to her room, then informed that she could order room service or dine in the dining room. Her meal was paid for, whatever she wanted, on him.

He was trying to give her the kind of romantic night every young woman should have when losing her virginity but without the actual man there for the romance. That's not what this was, but he wanted it to be a night for her to remember.

There was also a note waiting for her on the bed in their room, instructing her to be ready and waiting on the bed for him at eight o'clock sharp. He was spending his evening getting himself ready. He'd trimmed his mustache and beard and put in a washout dye to turn it from his normal grey to a darker color. He gave Braden a bunch of shit for dyeing his hair, but this was different. It was only for one night because he didn't want to be easily recognizable.

Damian preferred to keep his financial situation out of other people's business. The Ryder wasn't the kind of place he would normally frequent, and with his tattoos covered and all his hair dyed dark, he didn't look much like himself. At least not himself as he was now.

He looked a little like who he'd been when he'd met Anita. Looking not quite as old made him feel a little better about the young woman he was going to be meeting. He might not actually be younger, but hopefully, the age gap wouldn't be as noticeable.

Staring in the mirror, he hardly recognized himself.

When his phone rang, he jumped. Katrina. Should he answer? He should. Just because he was going out and doing something for himself didn't mean that he should feel guilty.

"Hey, sweetheart."

"Hi, Dad! How are you?"

"Good, how are you doing?"

"I'm good. I just wanted to call and say hi and let you know that I'm going to be performing 'My Angry Vagina' and 'Reclaiming Cunt' for the *Vagina Monologues*." The glee in her voice as she informed him let him know she was really looking forward to his reaction.

He held back his groan and rubbed his forehead.

"That sounds great, sweetie. I'm so proud of you." Which was true, even if he was also unsure about going to see her in this.

Katrina laughed.

"I can hear the enthusiasm," she teased. "I'm also doing some of the dialogue back and forth, but 'Woman 2' doesn't really have the same ring as 'Reclaiming Cunt.'"

"No, I suppose it doesn't." He couldn't help but smile as he shook his head, turning away from the mirror because it was odd watching his reflection when he didn't look like himself. She giggled again, clearly pleased with herself for discomfiting him. "Is that all?"

"Why?" Curiosity entered her voice. "Are you in a hurry to get somewhere? It's Sunday evening. I figured you'd be completely free."

Ah, shit.

Normally, he tried to keep her on the phone

longer, no matter what they were talking about. He'd tipped his hand because he was off his game.

"I... ah, have plans for the evening. Dinner plans."

"Dinner plans? Like a date?"

Thankfully, she sounded excited rather than upset. In fact, he was a little taken aback by how excited she sounded at the idea of him going on a date.

Hell. It couldn't hurt to tell her that he was. He meant to go on some real dates, eventually. This would get her set up for the idea of him being out there and looking. If she even needed that, considering she sounded more excited than he would have anticipated.

"Sorta. It's not a big deal. But, um, yeah, I've been thinking I might start trying to date." The words sounded weird coming out of his mouth, but they also came with a sense of relief.

Tonight wasn't a date. Not really. It wasn't about that. But it *was* the beginning of the next chapter of his life when he would be trying to date.

Katrina squealed.

"Aw, Dad! That is a big deal! It's okay, though. I won't go overboard... I'll wait 'til you have someone you want me to meet, but I just want you to know that I'm really happy you're getting out there. You deserve to be happy and have everything you want."

She wouldn't be saying that if she'd known how long what he'd *wanted* had been her best friend, but he appreciated the sentiment.

"Thanks, sweetie. I don't know that I'm going to be ready to introduce you to anyone for a while. This is all pretty new to me."

"I know, Dad. I just want you to know that I'm one-hundred-percent supportive."

"I appreciate that."

"Okay, now go! Have fun!"

Oddly, even though she didn't know what he was actually doing, it felt like she was giving her blessing to more than just dating. Like, the universe had known he needed some sign he was doing the right thing, that doing something for himself wasn't selfish, and that he could go enjoy himself.

"I will, sweetheart. Have fun with your rehearsals."

"I will! Love you. Bye, Dad."

"Love you too. Bye."

Hanging up the phone, he smiled, feeling a lot better. It was time to go get something to eat before he went to the hotel room where Sunshine would be waiting for him.

The anticipation and excitement that welled up inside him was far stronger than any of his reservations.

10

CALL ME DADDY

EMILY

Should her legs be opened or closed?

On the bed, propped up by a few pillows because she'd decided that was less awkward than lying flat on her back, Emily couldn't figure out what to do with her hands or legs.

Be waiting for me on the bed at eight o'clock sharp.

The directions seemed clear enough, but they were woefully incomplete. She wished he'd told her exactly what position he wanted her in, what she was supposed to look like when he walked through the door.

Pressing her lips together, she shifted, crossing one leg over the other, which caused the silky material of the thin white gown to slide away from her thigh because of the high slit. It was already practically see-through, but somehow, having her entire leg exposed made her feel even more vulnerable. She'd gone with white because she'd figured she might as well lean into the virgin thing, but she hadn't counted on how translucent the material would be.

She could see more than just the budded nubs of her nipples. She could see the pink of her areola when she glanced down at her chest.

Hopefully, he would like it.

Brushing her hair back from her shoulders, she immediately brought the locks forward again before glancing at the clock.

Two minutes to go and she still felt awkward and like she hadn't found the right position.

Closing her eyes, she took a deep breath, trying to push down the panic that had welled up inside her the moment she'd put the lingerie on. She didn't look like herself. Emily never wore clothing that drew attention to her curves, and she never wore anything this lowcut or thin. It felt like her entire body was on display, even though all the important bits were actually covered.

"I can do this," she whispered. "I can do this, I can do this. This is going to change my life."

Everything was going to be better after tonight. She just had to get through it. All signs were pointing to it being a pretty good night. Whoever Master D was, he was doing his best to take care of her.

Dinner had been amazing. She'd chosen to eat in the room, too nervous to be downstairs where other people were.

There had been a full array of beauty products waiting for her in the bathroom, and she'd had fun playing with the makeup. Something else she hadn't worn since the castoffs Katrina had given her had run out. Not that she'd ever worn much. Even the cheap stuff had been out of her budget.

She didn't know how much the stuff in the bathroom had cost. Wasn't sure she wanted to know.

It seemed a little bit of a waste to put a mask on over it, but she'd put on the makeup anyway. Just because. It helped her feel somewhat confident, a little less like plain, desperate, virgin Emily, and more like someone who knew what she was doing.

At least, she'd felt that way until she'd tried to position herself in a sexy manner on the bed.

Now, she didn't feel confident at all.

He was going to be here any minute. He was—

Oh God.

There was someone at the door.

Not someone.

Him.

It had to be him.

Her breath caught in her throat, and suddenly, it didn't matter how she was sitting or where her hands were because she could barely breathe, much less think or worry about how she looked.

The door opened, and her heart skipped a beat as a very tall, broad-shouldered man walked in.

Just like her, he was wearing a mask that obscured most of his face. For a moment, she thought it obscured his whole face before she realized he had a full beard. The black color of his hair blended in with the black mask he was wearing, which had thrown her off. He was wearing a suit that fit him so well, he looked like he'd just walked out of a movie—or someone's fantasy.

His lips curved in a smile as soon as he saw her.

"Hello, Sunshine." His voice was low, gravelly. Maybe a little familiar? Or maybe she was fooling herself. Sure, she'd met a lot of people coming through the diner and even recognized that one woman on the website, but that didn't mean she'd ever run into him before. Why would a man like him be eating at the diner?

"Hello, Master D." Her voice came out even higher and squeakier than it had for Tim, making her sound nothing like herself.

His smile flickered, then widened. Did he not like her voice? Shoot, maybe she shouldn't talk too much.

Or maybe she wasn't supposed to call him Master D? No, that was what he'd said to call him.

Maybe she was just a huge bundle of nerves who was going to second-guess everything about everything.

That seemed the most likely.

Master D prowled—yes, prowled; she couldn't come up with a better description of the way he moved—toward the bed, and Emily's breath hitched in her throat.

Oh God.

Her insides clenched... in a good way.

As he moved, he raked his gaze over her body. She couldn't picture what she looked like to him. She could barely feel her arms and legs, much less try to control how they were positioned, but the way he looked at her made her feel sexy. He looked like he wanted to eat her up... in a hot way.

"I've never done this before," he admitted, his voice even lower than when he'd introduced himself as he approached. His dark eyes blazed behind the mask, focused on her with an intensity that made her heart race faster and her nipples pucker. "But, if you have no objection, I think the best thing is to just jump right in."

"No objection," Emily replied, still squeaking. She couldn't seem to stop it.

He smiled again, reaching to cup her face in his hands.

"If you need me to slow down, say 'yellow.' If you need me to stop, say 'red,'" he murmured right before his lips touched hers.

Her lips parted under his, opening in shock as the electricity between them sizzled.

Safe words. He gave me safe words.

Thank goodness for the reading she'd done, so she understood what he was saying. She didn't have to think about it... and the fact that he'd given her safe words made her feel even better about the whole situation. No, this wasn't the way she'd pictured losing her virginity, but considering the stories she'd heard about how some girls' first times went, she was starting to think she might be getting a better deal than most.

DAMIAN

Sunshine was everything he hoped she'd be and more. She looked incredibly similar to Emily, even from what he could see of her face, but her lips were poutier, and her voice was completely different. Higher. In fact, he almost didn't want her talking, which was why he'd kissed her. It took away some of the fantasy playing out in his head.

Yes, he'd stopped being as drawn to Emily once he'd known about Sunshine, but now that he was here, it was more like the two were merging in his head—the fantasy he'd had for so long merging with the woman he wanted to use to replace that fantasy.

She'd been so pretty and unintentionally sexy sitting on the bed when he came in. He'd been able to see how nervous she was—and he hoped his own nerves didn't show. It had been a damn long time since he had sex and even longer since he'd had sex with a virgin.

Deepening the kiss, her tongue met his, and he felt the shudder that went through her as one of his hands moved around to the back of her neck, cradling her head as they shifted on the bed. The heat of her body pressed against his, and she moaned when he moved his other hand down to cup her breast, his thumb rubbing the silky material of her gown over the hard bud of her nipple. His dick throbbed against the tight confines of his pants, achingly hard already, the way he had been from the moment he walked in.

"Oh!" She gasped the word, high and squeaky, as he began to shift them into the position he wanted— her on her back on the bed and him above her, moving his lips down her neck as he filled his hands with her breasts. The silky gown was slippery against his palms, and he knew that would add to the sensations coursing through her as he squeezed and massaged the soft mounds, her flesh spilling out from between his fingers.

The little buds of her nipples were peaked, and he gave them small pinches, using the silk to stimulate them as he left a trail of kisses across her shoulder.

"Oh... Master D..."

His dick throbbed again, but it wasn't truly what he wanted.

This was his fantasy, right?

"Call me Daddy," he ordered, the words coming out in a growl.

"Daddy!" She squeaked when he yanked the front of her gown down, exposing her breasts, and closed his mouth over her nipple. He felt her body buck beneath his, shuddering from the sensations he was eliciting from her. He smiled inwardly.

Fuck, he liked hearing her call him that.

The need that had been driving him intensified at her lack of hesitation, her shuddering reaction to calling him Daddy. She liked it, too.

Fuck.

Her fingers threaded through his hair, holding him in place as he fondled her breasts, suckling and nibbling her nipples. His cock was hard as a rock, rubbing against the mattress while she writhed beneath him.

When he glanced up at her, it was almost jarring to see the mask rather than her face. Though he enjoyed seeing her lips, the mask took away some of his fantasy, and he refocused his efforts on her breasts.

Her body.

Making her moan and sigh. As she moved underneath him, the skirt of the gown slipped upward. He shifted, so he was more on his knees, no longer pressed so firmly against her, and moved one hand down to cup her bottom.

Felt her tense.

He squeezed, massaging her where her thigh met her ass, distracting her with new sensations. He wanted her overloaded on pleasure and need before he slid his cock into her, as soft and wet as he could get her.

When he moved his mouth away from her nipple, she cried out in disappointment, then tensed again as she looked at him where he was kneeling between her spread thighs.

"Relax, Sunshine, it's not time yet," he reassured her. "First, I need to taste this pretty virgin pussy."

Her sweet cherry pie.

Shifting downward, he draped her legs over his shoulders, the breadth of them keeping her thighs well apart as he pressed his mouth to her lower lips. With his arms under her legs, it was easy for him to reach up and continue toying with her breasts, squeezing, pinching, and pulling her nipples while she let out a surprised cry as his tongue delved between her folds.

"Oh! Daddy!" Her hips moved with her words, rubbing her pussy against him, his tongue sliding through the slick cleft.

She tasted like peaches and cream, with the slightly salty flavor that only a woman's body could produce. Delicious. Damian feasted like he'd been starving—because he had been. For years. He didn't want to stop. He wanted to lick and lave until she was screaming with an ecstatic orgasm. He felt his cock rubbing against the bed beneath him as he worked her pussy over with his tongue.

Fuck, he couldn't wait to be inside her...

Master D... *Daddy*... It was like something out of her books.

It wasn't just the money that was going to save her life making tonight special—it was him. She'd thought she'd no longer be a virgin by now, but instead, he was taking his time, kissing her, touching her, making her wetter than she'd ever been in her life. The feel of his tongue sliding over her most sensitive parts had her nearly sobbing from the sensations it elicited.

She was totally overwhelmed by the pleasure, the little bites of pain, the rising ecstasy inside of her. No one had ever made her feel this way before. She'd certainly never been able to make herself feel this way when she masturbated.

The sensations were crashing over her, her insides clenching. The eels in her stomach were completely gone, replaced by an aching, throbbing *need*.

"Oh, please... oh, please..." She moved her hips against his tongue and lips, then he released her breasts, shifting again, leaving her panting and whimpering, her entire body tingling.

"Good girl," he murmured as he straightened up, opening the front of his pants. His shirt came untucked at the same time, and she sat up to start unbuttoning it, wanting to touch more of him, to feel him against her. It felt like every inch of her skin had come alive... and she wanted him to feel as good as he was making her feel.

She wanted him to make her come.

"Fuck," he muttered as she shoved his shirt off and ran her hands over his chest. He had more grey hair on his chest than she'd expected and not a hint in his beard or the top of his head. Maybe men went grey there first.

She didn't mind. It made her think about Katrina's dad, which felt utterly filthy, given the situation, but maybe Master D was also a DILF. He wanted her to call him 'Daddy,' so even if he didn't have any kids, the acronym still fit.

A condom appeared in his hand—she wasn't sure where he'd gotten it from—then it was open, and he was rolling it over his dick. Which she hadn't gotten a good look at yet. That seemed wrong somehow. She should have taken a closer look at the first penis that was ever going to be inside her, but he was already pushing her back onto the bed, his lips meeting hers, and she knew it was too late. She would have to look later.

She didn't mind because she wanted it inside of her more than she wanted to look at it.

She felt empty. So, so empty. She needed to be filled.

The long, hard length of his body came down on hers, his warmth surrounding her, her thighs parting to fit him between them. She could feel the head of his cock nudging against her, and she shuddered with excited need, trying to move her hips to rub herself against him.

"That's it, Sunshine," he murmured. "I'm going to make you feel so good. I can't wait to feel you cumming all over my cock."

Emily whimpered, tensing slightly when she felt him begin to push in.

"Oh God... oh, Daddy... please..." She didn't know what she was asking for. It hurt. It felt strange. And it felt good, too. Like an itch she'd been dying to scratch, but now that she was, there was some discomfort.

He groaned, shuddering against her, and pulled back before thrusting again, harder this time. Emily cried out as she felt him move inside her, the slickness of her body assisting him in going deep on that first thrust. The slight bit of pain when he'd first pushed in was nominal compared to the growing pleasure, the intimate rush of sensation.

The kiss muffled her cries as he retreated and thrust again and again, going a little deeper each time. She clung to his shoulders, her body quaking from the unfamiliar sensations, the shocking intimacy of having a man on top of her, inside her. She felt so small beneath him, helpless against both his thrusts and the waves of pleasure that rocked her.

Her body ached, needing more, needing it harder.

She shifted, moving her hips up to meet his thrusts, her legs wrapping around him, so she could dig her heels into the backs of his thighs.

She could feel *everything*.

The rasp of his wiry chest hair over her nipples while he moved.

The press of his body against her clit every time he thrust home.

The way he throbbed inside her as he ground his body against her swollen lips.

The grasp of his hands as he cupped her bottom, tilting her hips toward him so he could thrust deeper inside her.

Her insides quivered and clenched, squeezing the thick length invading her, her channel adjusting to the new dimensions, stretching to accommodate him. She couldn't believe how incredible it felt to have him moving inside her, how right, how good.

Moving by instinct against him, she writhed with passion, her nails digging into his shoulders as the sensations began to sweep her away.

"Oh, fuck... oh, please... Daddy... harder... more..." She shuddered beneath him as her need rose, taking her closer and closer to the precipice.

"Fuck... Emily..." He groaned her name.

It wasn't until he froze, his cock buried inside her, she realized he'd said *her name*.

"Sorry, I mean—"

"How do you know my name?"

"Sunshine."

They stared at each other, his cock fully embedded inside her, and his eyes widened as recognition flared within them.

"Emily!"

No.

It wasn't possible. But she'd heard her name said in exactly that tone, exactly that way, more than once growing up.

She reached up and jerked his mask upward.

Maybe deep down, she'd known. Maybe her thoughts had been a hint that her subconscious had picked up on. She *had* thought he seemed familiar. She *had* thought he reminded her of Katrina's dad. Katrina's dad, whom she'd always had a crush on. Whom she fantasized about when she bothered fantasizing about anyone.

Staring up at him, her body throbbing around his cock inside her, trembling on the edge of an explosive orgasm that hurt because it was so close, the need only growing once she'd realized who he was, she could only whisper one thing.

"Please, don't stop, Daddy."

DAMIAN

Fuck, fuck, fuck, fuck...

His body moved in accordance with her wishes, even while his mind was shouting at him that this was a horrible idea.

Except... it was already too late, wasn't it? He'd already taken her virginity, even if neither of them had gotten off yet.

Emily was trembling right on the precipice of orgasm. It would be sadistic of him to leave her on the edge when she was so close. Cruel, even. If she'd wanted him to stop, it would be one thing, but she didn't. She said so. Then she moved beneath him, pushing her hips up to rub her clit against his groin, her no longer virginal pussy squeezing around his cock.

I'm fucking Emily. I just took her virginity.

Katrina's best friend.

My ex-best friend's daughter.

I popped her cherry, and now she's going to cum all over my cock...

The very wrongness of it somehow made it even more arousing. Damian's hips moved, thrusting into her, pounding harder and harder as he vented his emotions onto her body.

Emily cried out, shuddering, her nails digging into his shoulders as she came, her pussy squeezing the life out of his cock. He couldn't hold back any longer. He buried himself inside her with a cry, resting his forehead on her shoulder as he emptied himself into the condom. The only small barrier between them.

Fuck.

They both shuddered, coming down from the high of orgasm together, their breathing slowing in time. He could feel her relax underneath him, a small sigh escaping her lips.

What the hell is Emily doing auctioning off her virginity?

If she'd needed money that badly, Katrina would have told him, wouldn't she?

What if Katrina didn't know?

Don had always been overly proud. What if Emily took after him in that way? Or maybe she'd just been ashamed. That had been Elizabeth's problem. It hadn't been so much pride as the shame she'd felt at admitting how long Don had fooled her.

You won't know until you talk about it.

Yes. They fucking needed to talk about what had just happened and what was going to happen going forward.

What the hell had she been thinking? Does she realize how lucky she is it was me who won her? How wrong this could have gone for her?

And not in the way of accidentally fucking her best friend's dad. Who was still inside her.

Fuck.

He didn't want to think about how reluctant he was to withdraw from her, even as his cock softened.

"Fuck," he muttered as he did so. The condom clung uncomfortably, wet and cooling quickly as soon as the air touched it. His balls should want to shrivel, but when he looked down at her, his damn dick twitched, as though it thought it had a chance of getting back inside her.

It didn't. Of course.

He shouldn't have in the first place.

Little too late for that now.

He still had a job to do. Aftercare.

"Don't move," he ordered. Emily blinked up at him in a post-passion daze that did all sorts of things to his pride. Dammit. Now was not the time to be smug, even if he had achieved his goal of making her first time fucking amazing.

He'd been trying to make *Sunshine's* first time amazing.

But she was Sunshine.

Gathering himself, he went to the bathroom and disposed of the condom. The reddish tint to the juices on it made him feel a strange sense of possessive caveman-ness that he immediately pushed away. He threw the condom into the trash can and dampened a cloth with warm water, so he could clean her up. By the time he did, Emily was looking a little more like herself, nervously working her lower lip and blushing hotly when he spread her legs to wipe her down.

As soon as he was done, she sat up, curling her knees up and wrapping her arms loosely around them as she met his gaze.

"So, um, hi, Mr. Elliott..." Her voice trailed off.

"Call me Damian."

Emily blushed hotly again, and it struck him how reminiscent it was of their conversation where he told her to call him Daddy. Fuck. Was she thinking about calling him Daddy again? He was thinking about how much he'd liked it when she had.

Thankfully, he'd pulled his pants back up when he'd gone to the bathroom, so she couldn't see his slowly thickening length at the very thought of her calling him Daddy again.

They stared at each other for a long moment.

"What the hell were you thinking, selling your virginity on the internet?" The words burst out of him. He had no doubt she'd been a virgin before this evening. He still didn't understand how that was possible, but he knew Emily wasn't a liar and wouldn't try to fool anyone like that. What he didn't understand was why the hell she would do something so dangerous.

"Because I need the money!" She burst into tears.

"Oh, hey, honey..." It was not in him to deny her comfort. It didn't matter that she was naked—and he was still naked from the waist up—he gathered her in his arms, pulling her onto his lap as she cried.

Fuck.

Duh.

Dumbass.

He'd known the answer, even though he didn't understand how her situation had gotten so desperate that she'd needed to resort to *this*. No, what he really didn't understand was how she'd gotten to this point without him knowing about it.

Dammit.

He was angrier at himself than anything else.

Rocking her on his lap, he held her tightly until the tears ran out, then reached over to the nightstand to grab some tissues.

"Blow," he ordered as he held them to her nose. She did, sniffling a little, then shifted on his lap as she realized he was hard again.

Yeah, so sue him. His dick got hard when a pretty girl with no clothes on sat on his lap and allowed him to dry her tears. It had been a really long time since that had happened. All his Daddy Dom needs were bubbling up in a way that was hard to ignore. He knew he should move her off his lap and tell her to get dressed, but he really didn't want to let her go.

She's not acting like she wants to move, either. One more minute. I can have one more minute of this, then I'll move her.

12

HER BEST FRIEND'S DAD

EMILY

She didn't want to move from Mr. Elliott's lap. She also didn't really want to call him Mr. Elliott.

Daddy.

It was so wrong, but it felt so right.

God, what would Katrina think?

Even that thought didn't motivate her to stand. Though the wobbly legs didn't help, either. Her body still felt oddly out of alignment, as if she'd had an out-of-body experience and hadn't quite made it fully back yet. She wasn't entirely herself right now. The whole world had shifted on its axis just one degree.

"How much money do you need?" His voice was

much more contained than before, and there was no judgment, but Emily still cringed.

"I mean, none after tonight." She took the tissues from him, so her hands had something to do, playing with the soft folds. "You've taken care of everything I need and more." Which was when the obvious question finally made its way through her shock and embarrassment. "Wait... how did *you*..." Her head jerked up so she could meet his dark gaze, and her words stalled out as she was unable to think of a way to ask the question that didn't sound terrible.

He lived in the same trailer park she did, so how did he have so much money to spend on buying her? On spoiling her?

"Ah, well... I've done pretty well for myself, but I don't need much, and I like where I live, so..." He shrugged as if it wasn't a big deal. "Trust me, Sunshine, I can more than afford this weekend." His gaze turned curious as he studied her shocked expression. "I take it you and Katrina never talked about money? Not even how she was paying for all that school?"

Mutely, Emily shook her head.

The assumptions that had been made... she'd thought Katrina had a lot less money than she actually did, and Katrina had likely thought Emily had a fair bit more. She couldn't feel betrayed because both of them hadn't been completely upfront, but it was a startling revelation that there were still major things about her friend she'd never known.

All the little things Katrina's dad had paid for over the years... no wonder he hadn't been concerned about being paid back.

She felt stupid. And embarrassed.

Of all the people she wouldn't want to know her situation, Katrina and her dad topped the list. She'd known her best friend would want to help, but she'd assumed that Katrina would have her own money issues... instead, Mr. Elliott was apparently rolling in it.

Mr. Elliott took a deep breath, and his arms tightened around her, just a little. She could feel the thick bulge of his erection pressing into her thigh, and she felt her pussy quiver in response. It didn't matter that she was sore and embarrassed. Being on his lap, in his arms, turned her on all over again.

"So, what do you want to do now?" he asked.

She wanted to snuggle into the bed in his arms and never go back to the real world. Pressing her lips together, she looked down at the arm that was over her lap—and realized another reason she hadn't recognized him.

"What happened to your tattoos?" she asked instead of answering him, not sure she should admit what she really wanted. She couldn't imagine what he thought of her now, his daughter's best friend who sold her virginity on the internet.

"Coverup. Don't avoid the question, Sun—I mean, Emily." Despite his slip, Mr. Elliott's stern gaze bored into her. "I need to know what you want to do from here."

"Like, if I want to keep going for the night?" she asked. He blinked as if startled, and Emily bit her lower lip. "I mean, you don't, I don't, um..."

"I was talking more about how we should treat each other back at the park and when we inevitably run into each other when Katrina is home. But you want to keep going?" His hand caressed her hip as he asked the question, as if he couldn't help himself, and Emily's body lit on fire in response.

No. She should say no, right? This was her best friend's dad. Her dad's former best friend. The man had seen her grow up. Even without the age gap between them, there were so many reasons not to. And yet...

She didn't want to say no.

She wanted to stay.

She wanted to be in bed with a man who made her feel like he just had... a man who'd cared enough about a complete stranger to make her first time—after selling her virginity—amazing. A man who was still cradling her, touching her, as if he couldn't keep his hands off her.

A man who wanted her to call him Daddy, then backed up that title with everything she'd read about in her favorite books.

One night of this, a whole night, would be... there weren't words. There wasn't enough money in the world. Nothing would come of it, and she knew it could never be repeated, which was why she wanted it to last for as long as possible.

"I... yes... only if you want to," she whispered, staring back at him, unable to look away from his gaze. His fingers tightened their hold on her hip, and she felt his cock flex against the side of her thigh.

"I think we need to talk about what happens tomorrow." His voice had gotten lower. Gruffer. Similar to how he'd sounded when he'd first come in. But he hadn't taken his eyes or his hands off her.

"Same thing that would have happened if my mask hadn't fallen off," she replied, because that was for the best. "We go back to our lives. Pretend every-thing is normal. It's just for one night."

"And no one needs to know."

"How would they know?" The corner of her lips tipped up into a smile. It was reckless. Crazy. But it was also what she wanted. When was she going to get a chance like this again? Possibly never. So she wanted tonight, all of tonight, then she'd move on and never look back. She took a deep breath and played her ultimate card.

"Please, Daddy."

DAMIAN

Fuck.

She was going to be the death of him.

The right thing would be to remove her from his lap.

The right thing would have been to insist they talk about what happened now, then he'd leave her here to enjoy the rest of her night alone, and they'd never talk about this ever again.

But I'm already here. Is staying really going to make it any worse?

How would anyone know?

How would Katrina know?

He wouldn't tell her.

Neither would Emily.

Nothing bad had to happen.

He could finally fulfill all the fantasies he'd been having, the ones he'd thought to indulge with

Sunshine, and actually do them with the woman he'd been fantasizing about.

His hands were moving before he really had a chance to fully think it through. There was what he knew he *should* do... then there was what he *wanted* to do. Emily squeaked as she was manhandled from sitting on his lap to being over it with her butt up in the air.

If she was going to call him Daddy, she was going to get Daddy.

"Hey!" she cried out as her butt was tipped up. His palm came down to rest atop the curve, his other hand pressing against the small of her back to keep her in place over his thighs.

"You've earned a spanking, little girl," he said sternly. "Here's your chance to safe word, but if you want a Daddy Dom tonight, that's what you're getting, and your Daddy has decided you earned a spanking."

"Oh..." She said the word softly before wriggling a little on his lap. "Not too hard, Daddy?"

"That's not up for you to decide, Sunshine. Remember, 'yellow' to slow down or 'red' to stop," he reminded her. "Last chance." He caressed her bottom, squeezing gently as he waited, feeling like he was on pins and needles.

Emily sniffled a little, then nodded.

"Yes, Daddy, I know I earned a spanking."

Fuck me.

"Damn right, you did." He brought his hand down on her upturned bottom, not nearly as hard as he could have, but hard enough he knew it would sting. She squealed a little, jerking in surprise, but he kept going. The sharp slaps were firm, but she could easily take them. He could tell she'd reacted more out of surprise than pain.

"Putting your virginity up for sale on a website? Do you have any idea how dangerous that was?"

It took all his effort not to be too rough with the swats peppering her bottom as he spoke. She definitely deserved a real punishment, but he also didn't know what her limits were. He was pretty sure this was going to be her first-ever spanking. Elizabeth had told him that Don had never raised a hand to Emily —and Damian had had a very stern talk with Don when he'd found out how the man had been treating his wife—so he felt confident this shouldn't bring up any trauma, but since she'd never been spanked, this was going to all be very new to her.

"Ow!"

She squirmed on his lap rather than answering, trying to bring her hands up to cover her buttocks, even though he wasn't spanking her very hard yet. Heck, this was just a warmup. It didn't matter how long it had been. Giving a naughty girl a spanking was like riding a bike. He easily caught her hands and crossed them over each other, pinning them down just above her ass so he could keep spanking her with his other hand.

"Daddy, no!"

"No isn't your safe word. Say 'red' if you want me to stop. You were a very naughty girl. You know you deserve a far harsher spanking than what I'm giving you right now. You have no idea the kind of man who could have bought you."

Just knowing how close he'd come to not even knowing about the auction made him shudder. The idea that someone else could have bought her, someone who might have been cruel or worse... Fuck.

He started spanking her harder, and Emily squealed, squirming on his lap, but she still wasn't saying the words that would make him stop or even pause. She was accepting his commands. His dominance. Her punishment. Responding to it.

"Ow! Daddy, please! It turned out fine!"

Oh, that was absolutely not the correct response.

EMILY

Ow, ow, ow, ow...

The spanking hurt so much more than she'd been prepared for, yet she couldn't bring herself to say 'red,' even as part of her brain screamed at her to.

Especially when his next swat was much harder, the sting exploding across her already chastened skin. The heat was almost too much to bear, yet worse was still to come.

"Do you have any idea how lucky you were that it turned out fine? That I'm the one who bought you instead of someone else?"

He shifted his focus from her bottom to her much more sensitive sit spots. She shrieked as his hand came down on the skin between the curve of her bottom and her thigh. Her wriggling became much more frantic, so he tightened his hold on her wrists to keep her in place.

"You could have been hurt. You could have been killed. You are *never* to do anything like this again."

"I won't! I won't!" She wriggled frantically in place, trying to squirm away from his hand, which made her thighs press together. Inexplicably, she was even wetter than before, despite the heat growing in her backside. Emily felt several tears slide down her cheeks, but that didn't stop the embarrassing arousal that was building as a result of the spanking. "I'm sorry, Daddy!"

"Oh, I'm going to make sure you're sorry," he growled. "I might only have tonight to teach you this lesson, but I'm going to make sure you remember it."

More swats rained down now, peppering her entire backside, his palm coming down again and again on already heated skin. It hurt. It burned. And it made her insides clench and quiver in aching need. She was heating up inside and outside for two completely different reasons.

As much as it hurt, she wasn't sure she wanted him to stop.

"Ow, Daddy, I'll remember! I promise!"

"And if you ever need money again, you'll come to me."

Oh... no. Emily's breath hitched.

"Emily." *Swat.*

She shrieked.

"You. Will. Come. To. Me." He bit off each word as he spoke, punctuating it with another slap against her sensitive backside.

"I shouldn't need any more. I'll have enough after tonight."

"Say the words, *Sunshine.*" He spanked her on her sit spot again, making her squeal and buck on his lap. "I can do this all night if I need to. You won't sit for a week, and when my hand gets tired, I'll use my belt."

Oh, yes, please.

Except she was pretty sure she couldn't take that, even if some ridiculous part of her wanted it. Sometimes, the fantasy sounded better than the reality, as she was learning from the spanking that hurt so much more than she'd expected.

"I'll come to you..." Her voice trailed off.

His hand came down again, this time swatting her swollen, sensitive, recently devirginized pussy lips. The sound she made in response was nearly inhuman, unable to tell if she was in pain or turned on or caught in some unholy mix in between.

"You'll come to me if you need any money. Or anything. That is the one thing that is going to last past tonight, got it?"

Emily nodded frantically, blinking away the tears that had sprung to her eyes. Holy cannoli, that stung!

"Yes, Daddy! I'll come to you if I need anything!"

"Promise me."

"I promise!"

That gave her all the motivation she would need to ensure she never needed anything again. She would never want him to know that after all his generosity, she had somehow blown the huge sum she'd already gotten from him.

"Good girl."

With that, it was over. Emily sniffled as he pulled her around on his lap, manhandling her just as easily as when he'd put her over it, and she found herself with her head tucked on his shoulder again. It didn't feel the same, though. For one, the fabric of his pants felt a lot rougher against her swollen buttocks than it had before, and it burned where she was pressed against his thighs. For two, her insides were now throbbing in an achy way, as though he hadn't already given her an amazing orgasm.

The desire to have this night continue was now approaching 'need.' It didn't matter how sore she was; she wanted him inside her again. She wanted to know what it would be like with Mr. Elliott touching her, kissing her, fucking her while she knew it was him the whole time.

While she called him 'Daddy.'

Twisting slightly on his lap, she reached up to take his face between her hands—it was so easy to forget he was her best friend's father when he didn't look that much like himself without his head of grey hair —and pressed her lips to his. One night to take what she wanted... and she wanted everything.

13

JUST FOR TONIGHT

DAMIAN

Fuck, what she was doing to him...

Damian kissed Emily back hungrily, his hands sliding over her body, enjoying the softness of her curves pressing against him. His dick was rock hard and throbbing against her thigh as she kissed him, squirming on his lap. He could feel the heat of her bottom against his skin, and when he ran his hands down to cover both of her cheeks with his palms and squeeze, she whimpered against his lips.

He was going to have to remember to be gentle, which was easier said than done, but he wanted her to be a good sore tomorrow, not a bad sore.

Before his thoughts could go too far in that direction, Emily slid off his lap, falling to her knees in front of him.

Oh, fuck.

"I've always wanted to do this," she admitted, reaching for the opening of his pants, pulling it aside to free his cock. Damian groaned as she wrapped her fingers eagerly around the shaft, her wide eyes taking in the sight of his dick in her hand.

She'd always wanted to do this? What... give head? Or give head specifically to him?

He wasn't going to ask because one of those answers was guaranteed to stick in his brain in a way that would be hard to forget, and they only had tonight.

Assuming she meant she'd always wanted to give head, in general, seemed the safest way to go. And he was happy to indulge her.

She moved her hand up and down his cock, stroking him, exploring. Damian was happy to sit back and let her play, enjoying the sensations but enjoying her expressions even more. Seeing the way she was looking at him was giving him a new appreciation for a simple hand job, not to mention his dick. He couldn't help but wonder if his was the first she'd ever seen...

Which sent a certain primeval, possessive spurt of emotions through him.

Tonight only.

He was her first, not her last, and he needed to be honored by the privilege, then let her go. She would end up with someone her own age. Someone who wasn't related to her best friend. Someone who would damn well worship the ground she walked on. Otherwise, he'd answer to Damian.

Then Emily leaned forward and licked the tip of Damian's cock, making him groan as her soft tongue laved over the sensitive head, teasing the little slit. His hips thrust forward.

Emboldened, she licked him again, then opened her lips to take him in. Damian couldn't help but stare as she fulfilled one of the fantasies he'd been having for weeks—months—as her full lips stretched around his cock. Unable to hold back anymore, he stopped resting on his hands and sat up straighter, so he could reach down to fondle her breasts, gently pinching her nipples as she began to bob her head up and down on his dick.

What she lacked in skill, she made up for in enthusiasm, and she was a very fast learner... she was also going a little too fast.

"Fuck," Damian groaned, reaching down to grab a fistful of her hair, still caressing her breast with his other hand. "Slower, Sunshine, use your tongue... you're doing too good a job, and I want to enjoy this."

Immediately, Emily slowed down, taking her time exploring with her tongue, glancing up at him as she moved her head. He gripped her hair, helping control her movements, so she was going at the pace that he wanted, and he could see her pupils dilate as he did so. She liked that.

Shifting himself forward more, so she could get more of him in her mouth, and he could get a better hold on her breast and her hair, Damian groaned as her lips slid over him. The wet heat was glorious, her tongue sliding along the sensitive underside of his cock, teasing his head, then going back down again. Fucking heaven.

"Good girl... fuck... that's it, just like that." He groaned as her tongue worked, and she swallowed him deeper, gagging as he bumped against the back of her throat. Felt her mewl around his cock, pulling away, then he pushed her head back down, making her take it all over again. "Tap my thigh if you need to safe word."

But she didn't, even as he moved her head up and down on his dick, pushing deeper into her throat every time, making her gag and shudder. Damian pinched her nipple, twisting it a little, enjoying the vibrations of her cry across his cock. She liked a bit of pain with her pleasure, as he'd realized when he was giving her the spanking.

It had hurt, but it had turned her on, too.

And this was flat-out doing it for him.

Which was why he pulled her off his dick, leaving her panting for breath, eyes glassy, lips still open. She looked up at him, and he leaned down to claim her lips again, using her hair to pull her to her feet as he got to his until he could hold her against him while he plundered her mouth with his tongue. The hand that had been on her breast slid down her side, curving around to her back to cup her bottom.

Most of the heat was already gone, but she still squirmed and squeaked when he squeezed a handful of her soft flesh. He rocked his cock against her front, devouring her until he finally broke away from the kiss.

"How are you feeling?" he asked, releasing her hair and moving that hand down between their bodies to gently stroke her pussy. He could feel the slick arousal of her need on his fingers, and she shivered as he probed the tender flesh. "Would you like to try another position?"

Emily licked her lips, looking up at him, her eyes widening at the suggestion.

"Like what, Daddy?"

Fuck the things it did to his brain when she called him that. One night only. He had to remember that. One night, which meant he needed to sear all of these memories into his brain. He had a feeling he was going to be using his own hand and replaying them over and over.

"Like I put you on all fours on the bed and take you from behind, so I can play with your pretty breasts and ass while I fuck you." He deliberately made the suggestion fairly crude, just to see how she would react. So far, she'd seemed to like the dirty talk, and he wanted to test the waters.

From her reaction, the water was very warm.

EMILY

Oh, goodness...

"Yes, please, Daddy," she whispered. She loved the heat that flared in his eyes every time she called him that. It also made her pussy clench when she said the word.

She could still taste the salty, meaty flavor of him on her tongue, and as curious as she was about what it would be like to bring him to completion and swallow, she didn't know how many times a guy could get it up in a night. Older men weren't supposed to be able to as often, right?

Which meant that if she wanted more sex, she

probably couldn't really have it all. At least she'd gotten a taste of him. She knew what he felt like in her mouth now, what it felt like to be on her knees in front of him, running her tongue over his tip while he groaned and fisted her hair. She had even liked the gagging... because she'd been doing it for him. Putting up with the discomfort for him. Taking it for him.

She would have swallowed for him, too.

But she wanted to have sex with him again.

Priorities.

"Fucking hell, Sunshine." He cursed roughly, spinning her around so she was no longer looking at him. Emily found herself leaning forward over the bed, her palms flat on the mattress, holding her up. Daddy's hands moved over her curves, running from her sides down to her bottom, where he gave her a little swat that made her whimper from the little shock of pained pleasure that went through her in response. "You are such a good girl." He palmed her ass, squeezing the globes hard enough to make her groan.

"Hold still, Sunshine. I need to get the condom on."

"I got a birth control shot..." It was free at the clinic, but seemed like a spectacular waste when she wasn't having sex with anyone. She was grateful now though. She wanted to feel him inside her, skin against skin, wanted to know what it felt like when he came.

"Really?" His hand, which had been moving up to the small of her back, paused, as if he was thinking about her suggestion.

"Please, Daddy," she said, looking over her shoulder as she wiggled her butt at him. "I want to feel Daddy cumming inside me."

"Fuck me," he muttered, closing his eyes and rubbing his hand over his face.

"That's what I'm trying to do," she quipped, startling a half-laugh out of him.

It also got her another swat on her bottom, making her squeal and go up on her tiptoes. Her head snapped back around to face downward, her nipples tingling as she was rocked forward, and her breasts swayed beneath her. She wanted to feel his hands on her there again, feel his fingers pinching her achy nipples while he thrust into her from behind.

She wondered how different it would feel—if it would feel any different at all.

She wanted to know.

Fingers gripped her hips as she felt him pressing against her entrance. She whimpered a little because she *was* sore, but she was also slick and hot with her arousal. She wanted this. Wanted him.

In this position, she had more control over what

was happening—at least for now. She pushed back before he could thrust forward, impaling herself on him, and let out a little cry of pained pleasure as she was stretched open again. Muscles that had never been used before tonight strained, and she quivered around him.

"Slow down, Sunshine. Not everything has to be a rush." Rather than reaching under to cup her breasts, the way he'd said he would, he used his hands on her hips to hold her in place, slowly easing himself deeper inside her before pulling away. Emily whined and clenched around him, but there was nothing she could do to hurry him as he took his time, slowly thrusting back and forth inside her.

She could feel every stroke of his cock against her inner walls, the way it rubbed over that extra sensitive spot inside her, and the giddy rush every time he buried himself to his groin as the wiry hair on his body brushed against all her sensitive bits.

"Fuck, you feel so good." He groaned, reversed, then plunged in again. "I could fuck this sweet pussy all night long."

Emily whimpered, shuddering and squeezing her muscles around him. When he finally leaned forward, sliding his hands up to close over her breasts, she felt her knees buckle. His fingers pinched her nipples, tugging on them, pulling them back toward him as he thrust forward, using them to pull her onto him. It hurt, the little buds aching in his grip, but it felt so good, too.

He took his time riding her, playing with her, teasing her. Emily moaned, clenching around him, bucking her hips back up against him, but he didn't deviate from the steady rhythm he'd established. She felt like she was starting to burn up inside from the need, his cock rubbing against her so deliciously, yet not hard enough to get her to the point of culmination.

The need was growing inside her with every thrust, and the only thing she didn't like about this position was that she couldn't grind herself against him. Her clit was swollen, aching, begging for stimulation, yet the most she got was brushes of sensation against the little nub, which weren't nearly enough.

"Oh, please, Daddy," she begged, squirming back against him. "Harder, please."

The slow, steady pace was driving her wild.

"Since you asked so nicely," he murmured.

He gave her breasts one last hard squeeze, pinching her nipples between his fingers before releasing them and pulling back to hold her hips again. Emily cried out as he started moving faster, harder. The force of his thrusts made her elbows give way, and instead of being held up by her hands, she was now braced on her forearms. Her breasts swayed beneath her, the aching tips rubbing against the cover beneath her, stimulating her in an entirely new way with every thrust.

"Daddy!" She shuddered, her pussy clamping down on him, but in this position, it was easier for him to keep moving, the friction sending waves of pleasure through her, driving her ecstasy higher and higher.

"That's it, Sunshine, cum all over Daddy's cock."

Emily cried out wordlessly as her pleasure crested, and she found her upper body flat on the bed, no longer able to hold herself up as her muscles went weak from the rapture spreading through her. She felt Daddy's hands on her hips, holding her in place, pinning her against the bed, as the rhythm of his thrusts became wild, rough, slamming his cock into her over and over again while she squirmed in place.

The pleasure was almost too much to bear, and when he slipped his hand between her and the mattress, curving his fingers to rub her swollen clit, she screamed into the blankets beneath her to muffle her cry. The pleasure was too intense, an exquisite agony that exploded inside her, sizzling across her nerve endings and leaving her trembling and helpless in its wake.

She felt him thrust in hard, the rigid length of his

cock somehow feeling harder and larger than ever before. She felt the pulse of it inside her, the way it throbbed against her clenching muscles, then the warm jets of fluid that spurted inside her, filling her with his own orgasm.

Panting, pinned in place, shuddering from the aftereffects of her climax, she wished the night never had to end.

THE MORNING AFTER

DAMIAN

Watching Emily sleep, Damian resisted the urge to reach out and touch her cheek. It might wake her up, and that wouldn't be for the best, as much as he wanted it. He'd want to touch more than her face, and she had to be sore after last night.

After the second time they'd had sex, they'd gotten into the shower, and he'd cleaned her off... then gotten her dirty all over again when he'd had her ride him. Then she'd begged for a rest because she couldn't take anymore—and truthfully, he wasn't sure he'd be able to get it up again.

Not until this morning.

But they'd agreed on one night, and last night,

she'd been a virgin who went three rounds. She was going to be far too sore to do anything more this morning. Well, unless she used her mouth...

One night.

It was best to follow his original plan and not be here when she woke up, even though he thought he'd be doing it to Sunshine, not Emily. It might be even more important to leave before Emily woke up than if she'd truly been a stranger. They had their real lives to get back to, and for now, they were still living in the same place.

He needed to set the precedent on how things were going to go from here, and he couldn't do that if he stayed, used his mouth on her to bring her to another orgasm, put her on her knees to get *his* pleasure, then offered her a ride back home. Besides, the limo was going to be returning for her.

No.

It was better this way.

Staring at her, he tried to memorize the way she looked - the way the sheet was pulled tight against her breasts, the way her lips were slightly parted, her hair spread out across the sheets...

Forcing himself to walk out the door was the hardest thing he'd ever done in his life, but it had to be done. Once he was out, it was a little easier to walk down the hall. Once he was down the hall, it was a little easier to walk to his motorcycle. Once he was on his motorcycle, it almost wasn't hard at all to drive away.

Almost.

TWO WEEKS LATER

Looking up as Emily drove her new-used car into the trailer park, Damian couldn't help but smile. It had been a week since she'd gotten her money, and he was still watching her comings and goings, but in a completely different way. He was well aware that park gossip said she'd gotten a new job that allowed her to buy the car.

No one was aware of the windfall that had come her way or the circumstances around it, but people had noticed some of the aftereffects. Like the car and the new clothes. Mrs. Martine had also commented on how she now had a smile on her face more often than not.

It hadn't hurt that Damian had firmly told Mrs. Martine that Emily had a good new job in the city.

He wasn't sure if she did or not, but he knew she would soon enough.

She was keeping busy; that much was clear.

And he... well, he liked knowing he'd improved

her life. Liked seeing the car, the clothes, the smile on her face, and knowing it was because of him. He still couldn't believe how she'd kept her circumstances secret from him and Katrina, and he obviously hadn't told his daughter what he knew, but he was determined to keep an even closer eye on Emily from now on.

He also needed to get to the club again. Unfortunately, his desire to go to BDE and find someone to scene with, possibly to date, had died, buried under a pile of new fantasies.

Oh, he had gone. Once. Long enough to realize he wasn't interested in anyone there, and all he could think about was Emily. Still. Instead of the one night wiping her away from his brain, she'd completely invaded it. He didn't have to fantasize about how she tasted anymore. He knew. And rather than fulfilling the fantasy, it had left him wanting more.

His phone buzzed.

Mrs. Martine letting him know Emily had just gotten home.

It was funny—everything was the same, but everything was different, too. He still got the updates from Mrs. Martine, but Emily was driving into the park instead of walking from the bus stop. He was still obsessed with her, but his emotions had taken on a whole new flavor now that he'd had her... now that he knew she liked the same things he did... now that she'd called him Daddy.

He heard her voice in his dreams.

"Fuck," he muttered, turning away from the window. He needed to get his shit together.

Tonight, he was going to go back to BDE, and he was going to scene with someone else. Even if he wasn't feeling it. He needed to get himself out there and out of his fantasies with Emily. That was the first step.

EMILY

"Okay, what the hell is going on? What new job did you get?" Katrina's questions were more of a demand.

"Oh, you know, a job down in Charleston. In one of the offices there." The moment the lie left her mouth, she knew she was going to regret it because she couldn't just walk away from Katrina the way she did most of the people who asked. There was a reason she'd been avoiding answering the phone when Katrina called, but after driving past Mr. Elliott's trailer and seeing him there... well, picking up her best friend's phone call had seemed like a good way to remind her why she needed to keep her distance from him.

Daddy.

If it wasn't for Katrina...

That was useless thinking because Katrina existed and was Emily's best friend.

"One of the offices there," Katrina repeated, her voice heavy with skepticism. "Which office?"

"Verity Health."

"Uh-huh. And you didn't tell me that you'd gotten a new job... why?"

"Well, we haven't talked much..." Emily's voice trailed off, and she winced. She hadn't said anything to Katrina because all the lies felt somehow different with her. Maybe because of the things she now knew about Katrina. Maybe because she now knew Katrina's dad in the biblical sense. Maybe a little bit of both.

Shoot.

No wonder Katrina was grilling her.

If Emily had actually gotten a new job, Katrina would have been her first call. Especially because she'd already told Katrina about losing her last one, and she'd known her best friend was worried about her. But she'd gotten all in her head and weird about the money, and now Katrina had heard about it from someone else, and she knew something was up.

"Try again, Emily Graham. You are being all kinds of sus, and I am not buying it." A little note of hurt entered Katrina's voice. "Why don't you want to tell me? I know I haven't been able to be there for you like I used to, but—"

"No, no, that's not it at all," Emily said immediately, shaking her head even though Katrina couldn't see her. Darn it. She really hadn't been thinking. She'd been so thrown by her night with Katrina's dad, waking up to find him gone, then all the money that had come into her account and trying to figure out all of *that*, plus dealing with her lingering feelings... Normally, that would be the kind of thing she would talk about with Katrina. If only the man hadn't been Katrina's dad. But she needed to give her best friend something.

"I um... I sold my virginity in an online auction."

"You *what?!*" Katrina's shriek nearly blew out Emily's eardrums. She quickly pulled the phone away from her ear as Katrina kept shrieking at her, talking fast enough that Emily couldn't hear the words.

"Kat! Kat! Take a deep breath!" Emily yelled, thankful she was in the privacy of her own home. Sighing, she sat down on the kitchen chair, smiling when she felt the cushion instead of the hard wood under her butt. She was doing her best to be conservative with the money and only spending where she needed to, but she had gone a little wild at the local Walmart. New clothes, toiletries, a little bit of makeup, new sheets for her bed, cushions for the chairs... she was waiting for the mattresses to go on sale before she got a new one, but her day-to-day life had vastly improved.

She'd even gotten a few little pictures to hang over some of the most egregious stains on the walls, the ones that brought up the worst memories. Paint would work, too, but the pictures had been a lot cheaper. Once she managed to get a job, she'd invest more in getting her home into better shape, but for now, it was amazing just how much a difference a few small changes had wrought.

Katrina took several audible, deep breaths before yelling again.

"What the hell, Emily? Do you have any idea how dangerous that was?"

Like father, like daughter, apparently. Emily's bottom tingled with the memory of the spanking Mr. Elliott had given her—which was wildly inappropriate at the moment.

"I know! But..." Emily sighed. It was time to tell her friend everything about how bad things had gotten. About her panic when she'd been fired, about going to the strip club, about signing up for the auction to try to fix her life. So she did.

Now that she was out of it, it was easier to admit how bad it had gotten.

Not that she could tell Katrina *everything*.

"He wore a mask, and so did I, so we wouldn't be able to recognize each other."

"Well, that sounds smart. And he used a condom, right?"

"Right." The first time. But she definitely wasn't explaining he hadn't used one every time. The only reason she'd trusted him enough for that was because she knew him. She needed to quickly move on from this topic. "I fell asleep, and when I woke up, he was gone, and I was a couple-hundred-thousand-dollars richer."

Katrina blew out a breath.

"I still think you were stupid as hell, but I almost get it. Except why on earth didn't you tell me? I could have helped!"

"I figured you had enough things to pay for, considering where you're going to school and getting your master's and everything. Plus," she added before Katrina could start arguing with her, "I didn't want to be anything like my Dad."

Her dad had borrowed money from just about everyone in the park at some point. Sometimes, she wondered why her neighbors still talked to her, cared about her, considering the way her dad had been. But no one blamed her for his debts. A few of them had come calling to see if she could pay them back, and she had, but not because they'd threatened her or anything, but because it had been the right thing to do. They were definitely never going to see any of the money from her dad. She didn't even know where he was anymore.

"The amount I needed... it was too much, and I had no way of knowing if I'd ever be able to pay it off. Now, I don't have to worry. I paid all the bills, paid all the credit cards, and I still have a little bit of a cushion. I need to get a job, but I'm not in dire straits anymore, and I got myself out of it." She said that last part with pride because that was how she felt.

She'd fixed the situation herself.

Well, Mr. Elliott had fixed the situation, but even if he hadn't been the one to buy her virginity, the situation would have been fixed. She had just gotten an amazing night out of it, in addition to everything being fixed. It was still hard not to feel like she owed him, specifically, but she was going to pay him back by doing exactly what they'd talked about. She would take care of herself, and she would make sure Katrina never knew who popped her cherry.

"I get it, I do, but I swear, Emily, next time you *tell me*." Her voice lowered. "I don't talk about this much because my dad always wanted me to keep it a secret, but we have plenty of money, okay? My dad has paid for all my school. I have no loans. I don't work because he doesn't want me to lose my focus, and it makes him happy to pay for everything and spoil me."

Katrina made an aggravated noise before continuing. "You are my best friend. My sister from another mister. If you need a bill paid, you tell me. If you don't have food, you tell me. Or I swear I will come back home and take over your whole life and pay for everything until your pride is screaming and you're crying in a puddle on the floor. Because fuck your pride."

Pressing her lips together, Emily did her best not to laugh because she knew that Katrina meant every word of it. Tears also sparked in her eyes.

"I love you so much."

"I love you too, bitch. The next time you start letting your pride get in your way, you think about how *you* would feel if our situations were reversed."

The point sobered Emily. She would have bent over backward to help Katrina, even when she had nothing herself. At the very least, she would have wanted to know what was going on, even if she couldn't help.

"I'm really sorry. I am. I won't keep you out again."

"Good. Because you are nothing like your dad."

"I love you, Em."

"Love you, Kat."

She did. She loved Katrina so much.

Which was why she needed to let this fantasy about Katrina's dad go.

15

THE KITTEN

DAMIAN

"Hi there, Emily!"

Damian froze in place where he was crouched beside Mrs. Martine's trailer, trying to coax a tiny black kitten out of the thick azalea bush beside it. She'd heard the kitten mewing and had called Damian to come help her because she was allergic. From what he could see of it, it was old enough to be away from its mother but still a baby. It didn't appear to be injured, just shy.

If it was hungry, it wasn't hungry enough to come for the little saucer of milk he'd had Mrs. Martine bring out.

"Hi, Mrs. Martine, what's going on?" Her voice came closer, and he could hear the small hitch at the end of her question, which must have been when she realized who else was there.

Act natural, act natural, act natural.

"Hi, Emily," he said over his shoulder, careful to keep his voice even. Pleasant. It was the first time he'd actually said anything to her since that night.

"Oh, um, hi, Mr. Elliott." Her voice didn't squeak quite the same way it had when he thought she was Sunshine, but close enough, and the memory made his groin stir. "Is everything okay?"

"There's a kitten hiding in my bushes. I'm allergic, so I can't get near it, so I called Damian to come help me."

And he'd come, knowing Emily had gone out and thinking it was a good time to stop by. He hadn't expected her back so soon. But then, she didn't always follow the same schedule. Still, she'd been pretty reliable about being out during certain hours, making it seem as though she was working.

It seemed Mrs. Martine's thoughts were going along the same line as his.

"What are you doing home so early? You don't have work today?"

"Oh, um, well, I'm not sure that place is going to work out," Emily said. "But it's okay. I actually got another job offer today I think I'm going to take!" From the sheer joy in her voice, Damian knew that this was a legitimate job and not just a cover for the money she now had.

"Oh, good for you, sweetheart. What are you going to be doing?"

"I'm going to be a receptionist at an accounting firm, and they offer education assistance if I want to take classes in accounting, and they pay more than my current job... plus overtime during tax season!" Her enthusiasm built with every word out of her mouth.

Damian had to smile. Knowing he'd played a part in her being able to get that kind of job, to take that worry off of her, made him feel damn good.

He wasn't the only one who liked listening to her. The little black kitten he'd been coaxing for the past thirty minutes shot past him so fast, he jerked back in his crouch and fell on his ass. Turning to see where it had gone, somehow, he wasn't surprised to see the little stinker rubbing his cheek against Emily's ankle, purring loud enough, Damian could hear him from several feet away.

"Oh, aren't you a cutie," Emily crooned, bending over to pick up the kitten. The shirt she was wearing was a little lowcut and loose enough that Damian got a glimpse of the pale curve of her breast.

Fuck me.

Nope, his desire for her had definitely not been

eradicated by their night together. His mouth watered, and his fingers itched to reach out and touch her. He shifted to keep the bulge in his pants from being too obvious.

"Oh, look, he's chosen you!" Mrs. Martine said with delight.

"Chosen me?" Emily froze, and the kitten protested, bumping his head against the fingers that had stopped scratching his neck.

"Oh, yes. You're his person. He didn't budge for Damian, even when offered milk, but he came right out for you." Mrs. Martine laughed. "That's the cat distribution system at work right there."

"I..." Emily looked down at the kitten, then over at Damian. "I've never thought about having a pet before."

"It does look like he's adopted you. He didn't want anything to do with me." Damian picked up the useless saucer of milk and got to his feet, holding it in front of him for her to take. She did so and put it down next to the kitten, who sniffed it and turned up his nose. Brushing the dirt off his jeans, Damian's eyebrows rose at the cat's snobbery. "Huh. Well, maybe he just doesn't like milk. But he clearly likes you."

"I told you skim milk wouldn't work," Mrs.

Martine scolded him, shaking her head and pushing her glasses up her nose.

At times like this, she reminded him of his mom. Damian shrugged. It was all he'd had on hand. He didn't drink a lot of milk.

"Though Emily didn't need milk at all." Mrs. Martine looked at Emily. "That's how we know he's your cat."

"Huh." Picking up the little kitten, who seemed thrilled to be handled, she blinked. "I... what do I do with him?"

"Take him to the vet to get checked out. Get him a collar and a tag, register him with the city, and get him microchipped. Get food and toys, and a litter-box. A bed." With every item he listed, Emily's eyes got bigger and bigger.

"I can help you buy some of the things," Mrs. Martine offered, clearly thinking that Emily's reaction was due to the cost. Getting a new pet was always expensive.

"Oh, no, I've... I've got it. The new job is going to pay really well," Emily replied, cuddling the kitten closer. "I just, wow. That's a lot."

"It's easier than a dog." Damian chuckled. "You'll need to clean the litterbox, but he won't need walks, and he'll be fine being on his own while you're at work during the day."

"That's true," she said softly, stroking the kitten between his little ears.

Deciding it was weird of him not to, Damian stepped forward to let the kitten sniff his hand and give him a little pet, too. Standing so close to Emily nearly took his breath away. She huffed out a breath, peeking up at him through her lashes as she blushed.

Fuck.

He could only hope Mrs. Martine didn't pick up on the simmering tension in the air between him and Emily. Quickly stepping away, he brushed his hand off on his thigh and cleared his throat.

"Tell you what, I'll go get you the things you'll need for the first week or so. You go set up your trailer for having a kitten. You'll need to find a space for all his things."

"Oh... well, okay. That makes sense. I'll pay you back." The way she was looking at him made him take another step back because what he really wanted to do was take her by the hips and pull her forward. Getting this close to her had been a mistake.

"No, that's okay."

"I insist."

"Just let him pay, dear. There's no harm in accepting help." Mrs. Martine smiled benignly. "I want to give you some cash, too. Pick him up some treats for me. I might not be able to pet him without breaking out in hives, but I can still spoil him a little."

"Of course, Mrs. Martine," Damian said, smiling back at her and giving Emily a look. *See? People want to help. It makes them feel good to help. Let us help.*

She probably felt like he'd already helped enough, but it would be incredibly suspicious if he didn't offer to do something. Besides, he liked helping her. And it was good practice for her to accept help, especially from him, with no expectation of him receiving anything in return. He wanted her to know that she didn't have to repay him in any way.

Emily took a deep breath as he raised his eyebrow at her.

"Thank you both very much." The kitten rubbed his head against the underside of her chin, purring loudly, as if he could sense that a decision had been made. Her smile widened. "I guess I'm a cat mom now. I should think of a name for him."

"Let me know what it is when I get back." Damian needed to get away from her before Mrs. Martine picked up on the vibes around them. He gave them both a salute and started toward his trailer.

As first encounters post-taking-her-virginity went, that one hadn't been so bad.

EMILY

I have a cat.

This was the last thing she'd expected to happen today.

It had been a really, really good day even before she'd met her new little buddy, who still didn't have a name. She just couldn't think of a good one. None of them seemed to fit quite right, and he didn't respond to anything she came up with. Not that he needed to, but it wasn't like she loved any of the names.

"Darkness?" she said to him. He didn't lift his head or even twitch. He was completely focused on cleaning his front paw. "Faithful?" She'd loved that cat in the Alanna of Trebond book series when she was a kid. His ear twitched, turning back toward her, then forward again. Okay, so that seemed like a maybe.

"I wonder why you chose me," she mused, watching him.

It was nice having the company. The kitten had made himself at home immediately. Mr. Elliott had gone overboard on getting him things. She really was going to try to pay him back at least a little, even if she didn't pay him back for all of it. He'd already given her so much... and it was kind of hard to feel like she'd really earned it. Not when it had been the most amazing night of her life.

If Mrs. Martine hadn't been watching when he'd showed up with a car full of pet supplies, Emily would have been tempted to drag him into her trailer and beg him to do it to her all over again.

Please, Daddy.

A little shiver went up her spine.

Her cat seemed perfectly happy sitting and washing his paws. She felt a little weird about leaving him so she could go... pleasure herself. But she was probably going to need to get used to that. It wasn't like he needed her attention all the time.

Getting to her feet, she glanced around the main space to make sure everything was in order. He had plenty of water, and there was a bit of food left in his bowl, so she wasn't worried he was hungry—in fact, she might have fed him a little too much—and there was a little bed tucked in the corner in front of the standing lamp for him to sleep in. If he decided to get off the couch.

Right.

The kitten was as set as he was going to get for the night.

The newest present she'd gotten for herself—an e-reader so she could download and read filthy ebooks without having to store them on her shelf— was sitting right there on the counter. *Yes, please.* A whole world of Daddy Dom books had been opened up to her. Right now, she was tearing through Raisa Greywood's Holiday Daddy Doms series and enjoying being able to read about sexy Daddies... and picturing Mr. Elliott for every single one.

So, she'd go lie in bed, enjoy her current read, then pull out her toy when she got to the filthy stuff. It wasn't exactly what she wanted, but it was as close as she was going to get right now. Her imagination was feeling especially invigorated after getting to see him today and having him buy a bunch of things to spoil the kitten with.

There was just something so sexy about a man who cared about animals.

She'd just gotten into bed and pulled the covers up when she heard the knocking at her door.

It's him!

No, it probably wasn't, right?

It wasn't too late, but late enough that she couldn't imagine who would be at her door. Mrs. Martine always called out Emily's name when it was her.

Maybe he'd forgotten to get the kitten something.

Maybe he'd decided he couldn't stay away from her for one second longer.

Emily practically flew to the door, thankful that she finally had real pajamas that made her look cute.

The kitten looked up as she passed but was otherwise clearly unbothered.

She pulled the door open, breathless, and froze in utter horror. It wasn't Mr. Elliott at her door. The universe had gotten everything mixed up. It wasn't her Daddy—it was her father.

"Dad?" It came out as a question, but she knew it was him, even though he looked a little different. His hair had grown out to his shoulders, as if he couldn't be bothered to cut it, and was liberally streaked with grey. It was stringy and looked greasy, as though he hadn't washed it in a while.

He was wearing a button-down shirt that had seen better days. There were small holes where the pocket was sewn on, and one of the buttons was missing. When he smiled up at her—a cruel, cold smile that didn't reach his icy blue eyes—she could see how yellowed his teeth had become. Even more so than the undertone of his skin, which had deepened as well.

Even though she wasn't happy to see him, her first thought was to wonder when the last time he'd been to a doctor. He looked sick.

"Hey, Ems. Couldn't find the key. Thanks for letting me in."

And with that, her dad pushed his way back into her life.

16

HER DAD'S THREAT

EMILY

"What are you doing here?" The words had barely left Emily's mouth before her dad pushed past her, shoving his way into the trailer. She was so shocked, she let him. Not that she knew what she could do to stop him.

She'd never been able to stop him. Neither had her mother.

"What do you mean, what am I doing here? Also, I'm going to need a new key." He patted his pockets as he looked around, as if he was still looking for it. "Don't know what I did with mine."

"Maybe that's because you haven't been back here in years." Even as she said the words, Emily inwardly winced. The resentment she had against her dad had built up over those years, making it harder for her to hold her tongue, even though her memories told her that was a bad idea.

Her father turned toward her, the ice in his eyes growing as he paused to look her up and down, an all-too-familiar sneer curling his lip. Then he suddenly laughed, his mercurial mood changing as quickly as ever. Apparently, that was still the same.

"Missed me, baby girl?" he asked, holding out his arms as if he thought she would ever want to hug him.

No. But she knew better than to say that.

Instead, she braced herself and stepped forward, giving him as brief a hug as she could, tension running through every line of her body. The fact that she was close to the door outside gave her some sense of relief. As did glancing over to where the kitten had been only moments earlier and seeing he'd made himself scarce.

Smart kitten.

She wished she could do the same.

"It would have been nice to know you were still alive," she said as she pulled away from the hug, feeling as though she needed a shower. Placating her dad was the name of the game, though. Placate him, then he'll go away. If he left for another five years, that would be just fine with her.

The fact that her mom was in jail while he was still walking around free was patently unfair. She felt like a bad person for wishing it was the reverse. On the other hand, she wasn't sure her mom would have gone through rehab if she hadn't gone to jail... but if her dad had been in jail, her mom might not have felt the need as badly.

Still, it would have been nice to know if he was alive or not. She'd wondered, more than once. She still wasn't sure how she felt knowing that he was. Relieved in some ways, but she also wished he wasn't *here*.

"Looks like the rumors are true, and you're doing well for yourself," her dad said, looking around the trailer, taking in all her recent purchases. Emily stepped away from him, tensing again at his comment.

"What rumors?"

"Oh, you know, I hear things." He winked at her.

Her stomach churned with nauseous anxiety. Someone from the park must still be in contact with him and told him about her new job and the things she'd been buying.

That was why he was back.

He thought he could get something from her.

"I did just get a new job. It's better than the diner, but I'm not rich or anything." She made the statement as noncommittally as possible, hoping he wouldn't hear the fear or worry that was rippling through her.

If her dad knew how much money she had...

She didn't want to finish that thought.

She knew his greed would win over any care he had for her. They'd already been through that test, and he'd failed. Miserably.

"Looks like you have some extra money on hand." He smirked at her as he ran a grimy finger over the glass of a picture of her and her mom. It was in a new frame, and his finger left a streaky smear across her mom's face. Anger flared inside of her, but she pressed her lips together, taking a deep breath and pushing the emotions down. They weren't going to help her right now.

"What do you want, dad?" Like she didn't already know, but maybe if he just said it, she could get rid of him. How much could she give him to get him to go away without endangering her future?

"Wow, I can't even come to my own home without the third degree? You know, you get the nagging thing from your mother." He shook his head sadly. "This is my trailer, too, you know."

Technically, he and her mother both still owned it, but Emily was the only one who had been living in it. She was the only one who had paid any of the bills for it since her mom had gone to jail.

"I know."

"So, really, you should have been paying me rent all these years." He shrugged as Emily's jaw dropped open. "Tell you what, give me fifty thousand dollars, and we'll call it even."

"You cannot be serious," she sputtered, taking another step back away from him. Not because he was doing anything but because she didn't want to be anywhere near him. She didn't want to even be breathing the same air. As her anger rose, she wasn't sure she would be able to control herself and keep from doing something stupid.

"Well, I need money, Ems." He shrugged again, holding out his hands, palms upward, in insincere innocence. "And you've been living in my place, without paying rent, for far too long."

"I have paid every bill for this place since you left!" She clenched her hands into fists at her side. She'd known her father was a jerk, but this took the cake. The very audacity of him... yet she couldn't be completely shocked, as sad as that was.

Of course, that was how he'd view things. Everything *they* had was *his,* and the whole world owed him. Including his daughter. It didn't matter that he'd disappeared for years and hadn't put a dime of his own money toward holding on to the trailer or keeping the lights on and the water running. He thought she owed him.

"Yeah, thanks for doing that, but you still owe rent. Tell you what, you can keep staying here, and I'll give you a discount on the rent. You don't have to pay me back all at once, either. Let's say, two thousand dollars a month to stay here, and that will go toward current rent and paying me back." He crossed his arms over his chest and flashed a smile at her, as if he was doing her some kind of great favor.

Emily's nails dug into her palms, the small bite of pain helping her focus on something other than her seething emotions. Losing her temper wouldn't help. It never helped.

Her dad fed off making people lose it, like some kind of emotional vampire.

"You wouldn't even still have the trailer if it wasn't for me. I do not owe you *anything*." Saying the words felt freeing, even as a sick tendril of fear curled through her. So much for placating him. She knew it was the smarter move, yet she couldn't bring herself to do it.

She didn't even know how to placate him right now because if she said she'd give him rent, he'd surely be back.

It might be time to go get a new place to live.

Especially if her dad was going to be coming around. That wasn't how she wanted to spend her money, but she could. Her new job meant she'd be able to afford it. The idea of moving away from the place she'd always called home was terrifying, and she hated not having it here for her mom, but she knew what her mom would want for her—and it wouldn't include dealing with her dad.

The thunderous expression creeping over his face made her take another step back. She was even with the door now, and she felt her muscles tensing up, getting ready to run... wait, shit, the cat!

She couldn't just leave the kitten here with her dad, even if he had made himself scarce. There was no way she could leave a helpless, vulnerable animal within her dad's reach.

"You owe me *everything*. I'm the one who raised you, who put food on the table, who clothed and housed you—"

"You *and* mom, and *she* didn't gamble all our money away. You haven't fed, clothed, or housed me for years!"

"You will talk to me with respect!" Her dad advanced on her, shaking one fist up in the air.

Bile crept up the back of Emily's throat. Anger at her father and fear for the kitten kept her feet firmly planted where she stood.

"Respect is earned." She lifted her chin, her heart pounding in her chest at the pure fury that lit up his eyes. They were no longer cold; they were now hot with his rage. "If you don't want me here anymore, that's fine. I'll pack up and go, but I'm not giving you one cent of rent."

She probably should have lied rather than poking at him, but once she'd gotten started, it was hard to make herself back down.

"Damn right, you're gonna go."

"Fine, just let me go pack up..." Her mind was already whirling. She didn't have any suitcases, of course, but she could get everything into some trash bags and then... Mrs. Martine? No. Mr. Elliott.

Or she could just go to a hotel—

As she stepped forward, intending on going around her dad to her room, she got the shock of her life when he shoved her back. Her arms flailed as she stumbled, just barely managing not to fall, but her leg banged against the chair.

"Ow!"

"Get out!"

"I need my stuff!" She needed her kitten. She managed to retain enough sense not to say that because letting her dad know she cared about something was never good. Stuff she could abandon, though it would make her heart ache, but she could not leave the kitten there.

"It's my stuff now since you're not going to pay rent." Her dad started walking toward her, menace in every line of his body.

Emily's mouth went dry... but she couldn't leave without the kitten. Her eyes darted around, trying to figure out where he'd gone, but there were so many shadows and dark corners he could be hiding in, and he was so tiny...

"Fine, I'll pay rent. Let me get my stuff." Whatever she had to say to get past him.

Her dad paused, his eyes narrowing.

"You have fifty thousand dollars you can give me right now?"

"No," she said quickly. "I'll pay it back to you. Whatever. Just let me get my stuff."

It was the wrong thing to say. She wasn't sure there had been a right thing. Her dad moved toward her again, his hands reaching for her, probably to shove her out the door. She couldn't go yet, though. Ducking to the side, she tried to get past him, looking around even more frantically for the cat.

Fingers grabbed her arm in a painful grip, digging in, and she cried out as her father spun her around. He slapped her across the face with enough force, her head snapped back.

"Fucking little liar. Get the fuck out, you ungrateful bitch." He swung her toward the door, and she managed to get her hands up in time to keep from fully slamming into it. She cried out again, tears sliding down her cheeks from both the pain and her terrified panic.

The kitten!

She couldn't fight her father. She couldn't even stop him from shoving her out the door, where she went sprawling. Mrs. Martine's trailer was dark, and she was relieved. The older woman could get hurt if she tried to get involved.

Mr. Elliott. I need to get Mr. Elliott.

He'd helped with the kitten before. He'd said to come to him if she ever needed anything. Emily jumped to her feet and ran down the street, hearing her dad slam the door behind her, locking the kitten in the trailer with him.

SAVING THE CAT

DAMIAN

Was it cliché for a car shop owner to unwind at the end of the day by watching tv shows about cars? Probably, but it was what he enjoyed. Some shows he enjoyed more than others, of course. A lot of the time, he was able to sit and let his mind wander while the tv played. Sometimes, he'd end up sketching some ideas for paint jobs he wanted to do.

Today, he was having trouble focusing on any of that, though. The tv was going, and he had his sketchbook out, but when his mind wandered, it always wandered to one place.

Emily.

When he blinked and looked at the sketch he'd

been working on, it was no longer of a paint job. It was Emily, spread out on the hood of a car, gloriously naked, exactly the way he remembered her.

Fuck.

Ripping the page out of the pad, he quickly crumpled it. No, wait, maybe he should shred it. Just in case it fell out of his trash or something. *Hello, paranoia.* But he really didn't like the idea of anyone else seeing Emily naked. Not even a sketch of her naked.

It was better to be safe than sorry.

A sudden pounding on his door made him jump up.

"Mr. Elliott! Help!"

"Emily!" He dropped the crumpled paper on the couch and bounded for the door of his trailer, jerking it open. She was on the other side, wild-eyed, one side of her face red and slightly swollen. *Fuck!* He grabbed her, pulling her in so he could see her better. "Who the fuck did this to you?"

"My dad... he..." Tears sheened her eyes, and she gulped, obviously trying to catch her breath. She must have run all the way over from her trailer from the way she was panting.

"Come in—"

"No! My dad..." She choked, coughing, probably dried out. Damian jumped into action, leaving her standing just inside the door while he grabbed a glass and filled it with water. She was still coughing slightly when he handed it to her.

"Take a sip, Sunshine, and breathe," he said, rubbing her back. "Then tell me where he is."

Her father fucking hit her.

He was going to kill the man—as soon as he found him.

Emily choked slightly on the water, trying to gulp it too fast. When she pulled the cup away from her lips, some of the water sprayed because she moved it too fast, not that she noticed. She looked up at Damian, meeting his gaze with a kind of terrified hopelessness.

"My trailer. He came back. He kicked me out." More tears filled her eyes. "I had to leave the kitten! Please—"

She didn't have to finish the sentence. Damian was already moving, turning to put her behind him while he went and took care of Don.

"Stay here."

"No! I need to come!" She resisted being moved behind him, digging in her heels and pulling away toward the door.

"You're safer here." Plus, he didn't want her to see him kick her dad's ass. Don might be an abusive, mostly-absent asshole, but he was still her dad.

"You couldn't get the kitten out of the bush

earlier. What makes you think you can get him out of my trailer while dealing with my dad?" Emily shoved at him, trying to squirm around him.

Fuck. She made sense, and Damian would hate for the kitten to be hurt.

"Fine. But you have to do exactly as I say, okay? You get the kitten, then come right back here, no matter what's going on with me and your dad."

"Fine." Her lower lip trembled, but she was no longer trying to push past him.

Damian's chest clenched.

"Promise me."

"I promise."

Giving her a short nod, Damian turned around to head out the door... which was when he heard the shouts. They weren't very close. They were coming from a couple blocks away... then he saw the orange glow lighting up the dark night sky. Right where Emily's trailer was.

"What's going on?" she asked from behind him, then gasped in shock.

They both went running.

I'm going to fucking kill him.

It wasn't an idle thought anymore. He didn't mean he'd beat Don up. He didn't mean he'd hurt him. If he could get his hands on the man right now, he would put him in the ground without a second thought.

Emily's trailer was on fire.

Damian knew it before he reached the street, where the neighbors were swarming like ants—everyone was out of their homes. A few were just watching, but only because most of them had already advanced on the trailer, fire extinguishers in hand and were putting it out.

"Fire department is on its way!" someone called out.

The truth was, they probably wouldn't be needed to put the fire out. The many fire extinguishers on hand had already seen to that. But Damian didn't stop running because he knew what most of them didn't—there was a kitten inside there.

"Stay here!" he yelled at Emily over his shoulder. She still tried to follow him, but someone grabbed her and held her in place as he reached the open door. Was the kitten even inside? He didn't know, but he needed to at least check. Dropping down to the floor, he crawled forward. Small remnants of the fire still flickered in places where the powder hadn't reached from the outside, and smoke hung heavy in the air.

"Here, Damian."

Glancing over his shoulder, he saw Teddy, one of the guys who lived on Emily's street, holding out a fire extinguisher. Damian took it with a nod of thanks, then crawled forward, deeper into the trailer.

"Here, kitty kitty," he said, looking under the table and chairs. He coughed. He wasn't going to be able to stay in here long. He wasn't even sure the kitten was in here. It could have run out the open door. If it was smart, it would have.

A tiny mew caught his attention, and a little furry body came pelting out of nowhere to hit him square in the chest. Where had the damn thing been hiding? He didn't know, but at least it was alive. It purred, even as it shook against him, and Damian cupped the little guy gently in his hand, cradling him against his chest.

Apparently, it wasn't smart enough to run out the open door, but it was smart enough to know he was there to help.

EMILY

"Let me go!" Emily struggled against Rio's grip as she watched Damian disappear into her husk of a trailer. Black streaks marred its sides, the windows were covered in soot and powder, and she was sure everything inside was ruined.

"Absolutely not, Emily. You are not going in there. You'll just be a distraction." Rio cursed in Spanish when she tried to pull away again. "Let Damian do his thing. There's not enough room in there for both of you, and he told you to stay here."

And everyone did as Damian asked.

Well, not everyone, but almost everyone.

Emily pressed her lips together, tears sparking in her eyes. It was dangerous for him to be in there... but then it would be doubly dangerous for her to join him. Rio was right. She would be a distraction.

"Where is he?" she asked as Rio loosened his grip now that she was no longer trying to run into the smoking trailer. Her neighbors milled around, shooting her sympathetic looks, all of them relieved the fire hadn't spread beyond her trailer. She was glad about that, too, but she wouldn't be able to relax until she knew that Damian—Mr. Elliott... *Daddy*—and the kitten were safe.

"Give him a minute," Rio replied, trying to sound soothing, but she could hear the worry in his voice.

Going into the trailer wasn't the smart thing to do... even to save a kitten. She was never going to forgive herself if Mr. Elliott got hurt because of her.

My Daddy.

That's how she thought of him, really thought of him, ever since that night at the hotel. Right now, that's what he was being. Taking care of her, saving her kitten, she didn't feel like he was Mr. Elliott. That was too distant. Too cold. Right now, he wasn't being Katrina's father; he was being Emily's Daddy, and it made her feel a little bit safer, a little bit less afraid, to think of him that way.

If he got hurt because—

"There he is!" This time, Rio didn't hold her back as she ran forward and went straight for her Daddy while everyone else crowded around. Cuddled up against his chest was a tiny, black, purring ball of fur. "Oh my God, you saved him!"

"He's okay, just scared," Daddy said, lifting one arm so she could snuggle up with both of them, too. She didn't realize she was crying until she had both of her arms around him and felt the dampness of her cheek against his t-shirt.

"I was scared, too," she said with a sniffle.

Daddy rubbed her shoulder, making a small hushing noise, before he lifted his head, looking around.

"Has anyone seen Don Graham?" he asked in a loud voice.

The murmurs around them went silent, and Emily saw shock on more than one face.

"Did Don have something to do with this?" The

voice came from the crowd, full of horror, followed by several gasps.

"Very likely. He assaulted Emily before she came running to get me, and as soon as I stepped out of my trailer, we saw the flames." Daddy sounded grim, tightly controlled fury thrumming through his voice.

Emily tucked her head into his chest. She didn't care what anyone thought right now. She was just so happy he was okay and that the kitten was okay. She needed to be near him.

No one would blame her.

After all, her trailer had just burned.

Her breathing hitched on a sob as it hit her. Her trailer had just *burned*.

The sound of sirens filled the air, getting louder. The fire department was here.

Because her trailer had burned.

An hour later, Emily sat on Mrs. Martine's steps, watching numbly as her Daddy talked to the firemen. Yes, that was still how she was thinking of him. It was the only thing keeping her from falling apart. A Daddy Dom took care of his babygirl. And if he wasn't her Daddy, then she needed to be handling everything on her own, and right now, she didn't think she could. But she could lean on him because he was her Daddy.

Part of her brain, a more logical part, knew she

was making excuses, but she didn't care. She was a wailing, sobbing mess, and if she needed to think of Mr. Elliott as Daddy to get through the night, that's what she was going to do.

Mrs. Martine had her arm draped around Emily's shoulder, holding the blanket in place to help keep her warm. Not that she felt cold. She felt numb. Though at least her kitten was safe.

"Phoenix."

"What?" Mrs. Martine asked.

Emily looked down at the little black fuzzball. He purred.

"I'm going to name him Phoenix."

There was a small pause of silence.

"That sounds like a good name." Mrs. Martine patted her arm. "Because he rose from the ashes?"

"Exactly."

Just like Emily wanted to do. It didn't matter what life threw at her, or her father, she'd find a way through it. Emily lifted her gaze again. Daddy was on his way back to them.

"You can't go back in your trailer tonight," he said, not unkindly, but it was clear he was too tired to try to soften the words.

She'd already known that, but hearing it still felt like a blow to her chest.

"Okay. Is there any sign of my... my..." She couldn't

even say the word dad. Not when the man standing in front of her registered in her brain as 'Daddy.' There was also the knowledge that her father was responsible for the fire, one way or another. She couldn't think about that right now, though.

She couldn't think about her father, couldn't think about what might be destroyed in the trailer, or what she was going to do tomorrow. She just felt numb and empty.

"No sign of... Don." His jaw worked. He looked like he was full of the anger she should be feeling but couldn't find the energy.

"You can stay with me tonight if you want, dear," Mrs. Martine said.

"No. She'll go with me. I have the extra room, and just in case Don comes back..."

Emily shivered, and Mrs. Martine nodded.

"Come on, Sunshine." Daddy's voice softened as he held out his hand to her. She put her fingers in his and felt herself relax. "I'll take care of her, Mrs. Martine."

"Let me know if you need anything," the older woman said, getting to her feet and giving Emily a hug. Emily hugged her back. She was grateful for the offer, but she knew where she wanted to be—with her Daddy.

18

ONE MORE NIGHT

DAMIAN

Arson.

Fucking arson.

What the hell had Don been thinking? Had he known there was a cat inside or just not cared? Had he just been angry at Emily?

He didn't think he could tell Emily right now. She looked as if she was about to crumple into a million pieces.

He wanted to find the man and rip him apart limb from limb.

But Emily needed him more.

"Come on, Sunshine." Wrapping his arm around her shoulders, he pulled her against him and walked her and the kitten back to his trailer. She went easily, following his lead, slumping as though she was thankful he was taking charge.

At least he could do this for her. His Daddy Dom instincts had gone into overdrive. Emily needed him, and everything in him responded to that. Even without their night together, he would have stepped in to help her. The fact he felt possessive over her as well as protective... well, it added another dimension to his emotions.

She moved on autopilot. He sat her down on his couch while he got a makeshift litterbox together for the kitten as well as a little bed. They'd have to get him some more food in the morning. Looking around, he couldn't think of anything else he could do for the kitten right now, which meant it was time to handle Emily.

Still sitting on the couch, she was staring down at the kitten in her lap, who was happily purring and cleaning himself, apparently unbothered by his adventures. As far as Damian could tell, he wasn't hurt or distressed. Brave little thing.

"I've got everything set up for the kitten—"

"Phoenix," she interrupted him. Damian paused, blinking, and she looked up. "I named him Phoenix."

"That's a good name." And very appropriate. Damian kept his tone gentle. "It's time to put him down and get ready for bed. Here." He picked up

Phoenix and placed him in the nest of blankets he'd put together for a kitten bed. Emily blinked as if seeing the bed for the first time, then immediately burst into tears.

Fuck.

He'd been trying to keep his hands to himself as much as he could, but there was no way he could ignore her crying. Sliding next to her on the couch, he pulled her onto his lap, rubbing her back and murmuring reassurances that everything would be okay while he let her cry it out. He wasn't really trying to stop her tears—she needed the emotional release—but he wanted to be there to support her.

She cried hard for the first few minutes before her sobs began to slow, her head leaning against his shoulder, breath hiccupping.

"That's it, Sunshine. I've got you." He cuddled her close, thankful his dick was behaving, even though she was on his lap. The last thing she needed right now was a horny bastard trying to take advantage of her emotional upheaval and pushing himself on her.

"How could he?" she asked, choking the words out through sniffles.

Damian tightened his arms around her. He didn't have an answer for her because he didn't know how her father could have, either. Twenty years ago, he would have said that Don would never do such a thing, but he didn't know the man anymore. He'd changed beyond all recognition.

"I don't know," he finally said. "There's something wrong with him. Did he say why he came back?"

Emily sniffled.

"Someone told him about my new job or something, or maybe they noticed all the things I've been buying. He told me he needed money, that I owe him rent." She sounded more angry than sad now, her righteous frustration coming through in her voice. "I'm the one who kept the trailer from being repossessed after mom was arrested and he left! I told him I don't owe him anything and... well, we fought." Her voice hitched, turning sad again.

Damian held back his own curse. Considering the handprint on her cheek when she'd knocked on his door, he could guess how that fight had gone.

"Maybe he needs the insurance money." He didn't think before he spoke, and he felt Emily go still in his arms.

"Would he really burn down our home just to get insurance money?" Her voice quavered.

Damian sighed. Stroking her hair, he pulled it away from her neck and rested his chin on top of her head. He wished he hadn't said that out loud. The fact that money meant more to Don than his daughter wasn't something she needed rubbed in her face, even if it was probably true.

"He hasn't been back in years," he pointed out gently. "He probably doesn't think of it as home anymore. I wouldn't be surprised if he still had some kind of insurance on it. If he was asking you for money, then burned it, that's probably why." Though he couldn't really be stupid enough to think that the insurance company would pay out when the fire was due to arson, was he? Then again, it was Don. He might be. Or he'd just been pissed and not thinking rationally. Anything was possible.

"I'm so mad at him, I could just…"

Emily made some small movement, but since she was on his lap, Damian couldn't really see what she was doing. He imagined she was miming something violent. He felt the same way. Then she sagged again.

"I'm not sure what I'm going to do now."

"You're going to stay here with me, and we'll figure it out."

"Here?" She sat up suddenly, twisting slightly in his lap, turning to face him with wide eyes still glistening from her tears. There was an oddly wistful expression on her face, and she looked at him like she was trying to figure out if he meant it.

Hell, yes, he meant it. She couldn't stay in her place, obviously, and he didn't want her leaving the trailer park. Then he wouldn't be able to keep an eye on her. Plus, this way, if her dad came back, she'd be protected. She wouldn't be alone. And if her dad did come back, then Damian could go ahead and kill him.

"Yes, here. Katrina won't mind you using her room." As soon as he stated his intentions, her face fell. Dammit. His chest ached in response, but it was the right decision. The right thing to do. He couldn't take advantage of this situation. He'd already done that once, and if he had her in his own bed, he wasn't sure he'd be able to let her out of it again. Though having her so close was going to be its own special brand of torture.

"Tonight... can I stay in yours?"

EMILY

If he turned her down, she'd run to Katrina's room and cry her eyes out all over again before licking her wounds and never, ever, asking for anything like this again. He didn't want to turn her down, though. She could see it in his eyes. Feel it as his cock hardened against her bottom.

He didn't answer immediately, but she could see him thinking it through.

"Please, Daddy?" she asked, deliberately not playing fair. She didn't want him thinking. She wanted him to touch her. And she could tell he wanted to touch her. His fingers flexed against her thigh and side, and she squirmed on his lap, rubbing her butt against his thickening erection. "One more night. I just... I need..." She wasn't sure how to vocalize what she needed.

Wasn't sure she could find the words.

But she felt it.

Craved it.

Another night under his care. Something to erase the events of the evening, or at least make it so that tonight was more than the night her father burned her home down. A faint hint of smoke clung to Mr. Elliott, but all it did was make her want him more. He'd gone into the fire for her kitten. He was a hero.

"One more night." It came out guttural. Rough. As though he wasn't sure he was making the right choice.

Emily wasn't going to let him change his mind or regret it. Brazenly, she pressed her lips against his, letting him feel her relief. She melted against him as he kissed her back, taking control. His hand slid up her back, fingers caressing her neck until they tangled in her hair and gripped the thick mass of it at the base of her skull. Emily moaned against his kiss, her tongue dueling with his.

Then he released her hair and shifted. She shrieked, pulling away from the kiss as he got to his feet, one arm beneath her knees, the other wrapped securely around her back, lifting her as if she weighed as much as the kitten.

Crap on a cracker!

This was the kind of thing she'd fantasized about but never thought would actually happen. Thanks to the books she read, she knew better than to tell him she was too heavy and to put her down, even if the thought ran through her mind.

Besides, he didn't disappoint, manfully striding down the hallway and turning her so he could push his bedroom door open with his shoulder. Emily clung to his neck as he carried her into his room. It wasn't a huge room, so the bed was right there, and he immediately placed her down on it, his body sliding down atop hers, their noses only a few inches apart.

"Last chance." He growled the words, sending a shiver down her spine.

"Please, Daddy, I need this." She needed him.

He groaned, lowering his mouth to claim her lips again. She kissed him back enthusiastically, arching her back to rub herself against him as she wound her legs around his thighs. She could feel the thick ridge of his erection pressing against her core through their clothing. Whimpering, she squirmed and rubbed herself against it, feeling the heat and arousal rush through her, replacing the fear and sadness that were riding her.

Sliding his hands over her body, he hooked his fingers into her shirt and ended their kiss long enough to pull it up over her head, then his lips were on hers again. She arched upward so he could reach behind her, his fingers seeking the clasp of her bra… and with one quick movement, he undid it with one hand. Considering he didn't have much room to work with, it was particularly impressive.

He shifted atop her, pulling the bra off her arms and tossing it to the side before filling his hands with her breasts. Emily gasped against his lips as her senses buzzed, her nipples tightening against the sensation of his callused thumbs rubbing over them.

It felt so good.

It felt so right.

Reaching up, she slid her fingers into his thick hair and gently tugged. Now, it was his turn to groan, rocking his hips against her, then he released her breasts and grabbed her wrists.

"I can't have you touching me, or I won't be able

to take my time the way I want to," he murmured, more to himself than to her.

Emily stared up at him, feeling both excited and vulnerable as she realized she was half-naked in his bed, his hands wrapped around her wrists and pinning them down beside her head. The helplessness of her position excited her even more.

Something flickered through his eyes, then he moved her hands up above her head, so he could grasp both of her wrists in one hand.

"Oh..." Emily sucked in a breath of surprise at how incredibly sexy the move felt, especially when he leaned over to open up his nightstand and pulled out a pair of metal cuffs. He gave them a doubtful look, then faced her again.

"These aren't what I would want to use—my asshole brother gave them to me last year as a joke—but they're what I've got right now." He closed one around her left wrist, the metal cold against her skin. Just feeling that cold loop around her wrist made her feel trapped in the most delicious way.

Trapped beneath him.

Trapped in his bed.

Unable to stop him from doing anything he wanted with her.

And there was a lot she wanted him to do.

Daddy threaded the cuff around the center pole

of his headboard, then snapped it shut around her other wrist, cuffing her to the bed. Looking down at her, his eyes blazed hot with need.

"Be careful. I don't want to see a single mark on your wrists from those, so no pulling on them."

"Or what?" she challenged, her heart beating a little faster in her chest as her insides clenched.

Not bothering to answer, he smiled down at her, then lowered his mouth to her breasts. Emily gasped, shuddering as his hands plumped the soft mounds, pushing them up and together while her nipple was sucked into his hot mouth. Pure pleasure shot through her, straight to her pussy, and she whimpered. Metal clanged against metal as she instinctively tried to move her arms, only to be caught up short by the cuff.

Daddy nipped her nipple, hard enough to make her cry out.

"What did I just say?"

"Sorry, Daddy. I couldn't help it."

"Not a bruise," he growled. "Or you'll regret it."

Emily wrapped her fingers around the bar and held on for dear life as Daddy's head dropped down to her breasts again.

19

BEING DADDY'S GIRL

DAMIAN

She tasted just as good as he remembered.

And without coming off of years of celibacy, he didn't feel so rushed. Sucking on each pert nipple, he enjoyed Emily writhing and moaning beneath him in his bed, the way he'd fantasized about for so long. Maybe this was what he really needed to work her out of his system.

It hadn't been the same at the hotel because it hadn't been close enough to his fantasy.

Or maybe he was lying to himself because that was what he wanted to do right now. He didn't want to admit to himself how right it felt to have her beneath him in his bed. How complete it made him feel, as though everything in his life was exactly where it was supposed to be.

"Oh... Daddy... please..." She rubbed her legs against him as she whimpered, trying to pull him farther up her body. With his lower chest against her lower body, she couldn't quite get the stimulation she was obviously craving.

Rather than answer, Damian began to move farther south, forcing her legs to fall back down to the bed. The handcuffs rattled against the pole they were wrapped around as he did so. He was going to have to go get her some nice leather cuffs.

No! One more night only.

But I should get some leather cuffs.

For whoever I date in the future.

These handcuffs aren't meant for this.

Which was exactly why his former police officer twin had given them to him. A little reminder from his 'big brother' not to break too many rules. Damian got a kick out of using them to secure Emily to his bed. His twin would not approve, which made it all the more delicious... as long as they didn't end up bruising her.

Pulling her pants over her hips, he tossed them to the side as well, leaving her completely naked, cuffed to his bed. Damian paused for a moment to run his eyes over her, trying to memorize how damn good she looked like this.

It doesn't have to be just one night.

You could have more nights like this.

Then you could see it every night instead of having to remember.

But no.

She was too young for him.

And even if he got over that mental hurdle, there was still Katrina to consider.

Tonight only. Because she was a subbie in need.

Tomorrow night, she'd be in Katrina's room, and that would be that. This was a circumstantial exception, not to be repeated.

Moving his mouth over her soft curves, he felt her squirm beneath him as he focused on her stomach. Society might tell her that the plump flesh was unattractive, but he loved it. Loved her softness, loved her curves, and told her so with his mouth... before finally moving lower to dip his head between her thighs.

"Daddy!" She squealed the word as he slid his tongue between her folds, licking her from the bottom to the top, flicking the tip against the little nub of her swollen clit. "Oh... please..."

Using his shoulders to push her legs up where he wanted them, giving him full access to the sweet folds of her pussy, Damian let her moans and whimpers wash over him as he feasted. Licking the outer edges, he worked his way inward, back to her clit, and circled it with his tongue.

"Oh, yes… oh, please…" Emily squirmed, her hips moving up and down as she rubbed herself against his mouth and tongue, shuddering from the sensations. The headboard creaked, and he knew she was holding on to it, which should protect her wrists. That knowledge allowed him to relax and focus the way he truly wanted to.

With her legs draped over his shoulders, heels digging into his back, he was able to reach around the sides to bring his hands up to her breasts. Digging his fingers into her soft flesh, he buried his face between her thighs as his hands went to work, pinching and twisting her nipples while he pleasured her with his tongue.

One last night.

He was going to make it a night to remember.

He savored the flavor of her, the sweet tang of her cream coating his tongue as he lapped up her arousal. She moaned, arching, as he pinched her nipples hard, adding a bite of pain to her growing ecstasy. He could hear the change in her voice as her climax came closer… but he wasn't ready for her to cum yet.

Changing up his movements, he licked around her

clit to tease her again, enjoying her little cry of pleasure, before he gave her nipples one last little twist and pulled his hands away to slide them up the backs of her thighs. Bending her in half, he pushed her knees against her breasts, giving him access to an entirely new area.

When the tip of his tongue touched the crinkled opening of her bottom, she cried out again, and he heard the clang of the metal as she reacted.

"Oh, Daddy, no!"

He lifted his head long enough to reply.

"Your safe word is 'red,' Sunshine, and unless I hear it, I'm going to lick this pretty little asshole as much as I want, then I'm going to put my fingers in there while I make you cum on my tongue." Just saying the words made his cock throb. As much as he wanted to take that virginity as well... it wasn't his to have.

She couldn't be his. Not really.

But he could have this.

Be the first to taste her. The first to touch her there. The first to make her cum while her forbidden entrance was full of his fingers.

She closed her eyes and shook her head, pressing her lips together, but she didn't say her safe word. She didn't even ask him to slow down.

Damian lowered his head again... and feasted.

❦

EMILY

Wrong... this is wrong... it's so wrong...

Then why did it feel so good?

She'd read about this in her books, but she'd thought it was only in books. Just fiction. No one in real life would ever actually use their tongue... there.

But Daddy was.

And it felt so good.

So many little nerve endings that she'd never known she had, all of them fizzing new sensations through her as her pussy clenched with arousal. And there was nothing she could do to stop him because she was cuffed to his bed, which made the whole situation even hotter. She couldn't do a thing to stop him as he had his way with her body.

Even though she knew she had a safe word, she didn't feel like this was an appropriate use of it. It wasn't that she didn't like what he was doing. It wasn't that she truly wanted him to stop.

It was just so *wrong*.

Yet when his tongue began to move away, she felt disappointment... right up until he was licking her pussy again, lifting only to briefly swipe a finger through her cream, lubricating it, before it moved lower.

"Oh! Daddy!" Emily squirmed, clenching as his finger pushed into the little hole.

His finger felt *huge.*

No way could something even bigger fit there. The stretching sensation stung, though Daddy's tongue helped relieve some of the discomfort. His finger kept pushing, thrusting in and out as if he was fucking her with it, while he went to town on her pussy. The handcuffs jangled against the metal frame as she squirmed against his mouth, her muscles clenching around the finger moving back and forth inside her, stretching open her tiny hole.

It felt even more wrong than his tongue had, an invasion into her body she couldn't quite describe, yet she didn't want him to stop. Her toes curled as pleasure surged inside her, stroked higher by the finger thrusting into her. As if he could sense the oncoming precipice, Daddy shifted all of his attention to her clit.

The hot, hard suction surrounding the sensitive organ made her body jerk upward. He wrapped his arm over her hip, holding her in place so he could keep suckling her clit, flicking it with his tongue while pure erotic bliss exploded inside her. All the while, his finger moved within her, sending her soaring as she squeezed and quaked under the onslaught.

"Daddy! Oh God, Daddy!" It felt as though she could levitate above the bed, but he and the cuffs were holding her down.

He shifted atop her, sliding his finger out of her as she went limp, panting and shuddering as she descended from the sensual high. Not that he gave her long to do so. Stripping off his clothes in a few swift movements, he nestled himself between her thighs, running his hand around the outside of her thigh and hooking it upward so he could press his fingers against her bottom again while rubbing the tip of his cock along the seam of her pussy.

Already feeling overstimulated, she gasped as he began to push in with both his cock and his finger again.

So full... the combination made her feel so full.

All the while, he stared down at her, watching every minute change in her expression as he sank into her. She felt utterly helpless beneath him as he began to thrust, his finger holding her in place. Her hands unable to reach up and touch him, all she could do was take his cock as he began to pound into her. With her slick, swollen flesh extra sensitive after her previous orgasm, the increase in sensation bordered on the edge of painful.

But she'd bear it. For him.

She wanted him inside her... deeper, harder. Wrapping her legs around his hips, she moved up to meet him, whimpering as the hot sensations sizzled over her. Agony and ecstasy clashed inside her, the over-sensitization of her most sensitive parts turning her into a mewling mess of pain and pleasure.

As if sensing the issue, he started moving harder, faster, his finger pushing deeper inside her. She could feel it rubbing against his cock from inside of her, an utterly odd yet wildly exciting sensation that sent her need climbing higher.

"That's it, Sunshine. I want to see you cum all over Daddy's cock."

"Oh God..." She tightened down around him, shuddering at his words as they pushed her closer to a second, stronger climax. She could feel the buildup, the pleasure rocking through her, bringing her closer and closer. "Daddy... Oh, yes... Daddy!"

It started deep inside, a wave of passion that rolled over her, pulling her under like a riptide and drowning her in pure rapture. Daddy groaned, slamming into her as she clenched around him, the slickness of her pussy allowing him to keep moving despite her spasming muscles. He felt bigger than ever as she clamped down around him, her body desperately trying to hold him in place as the onslaught of sensations overwhelmed her.

Emily cried out wordlessly as he thrust into her, again and again, lost in the maelstrom of agonized ecstasy. The pleasure was too intense, too sharp, too *much*. She was lost in the current when he finally slammed home, emptying himself into her, and she spasmed around him. Darkness shimmered on the edges of her vision, threatening to pull her under.

It was the jangling of metal cuffs against a metal bed frame that helped her swim up out of it just as Daddy huffed and slumped over her. His finger slid out of her, leaving her feeling a little bit empty, even as he rocked gently against her swollen lips and clit, sending small aftershocks of pleasure rippling over her.

He groaned, shuddering against her, pulsing inside her.

"Good girl, Sunshine," he murmured.

❦ 20 ❦

CAUGHT

DAMIAN

It was the soft feeling of a woman against him that woke him.

He knew he was in his own bed, which was why a woman there with him didn't make sense. But he woke up wrapped around one. Soft curves pressed against his ragingly hard cock, which was nestled between the cheeks of her ass. His arm was draped over her, his fingers curled around one breast. The faint scent of lavender tickled his nose from where it was buried in her hair, accompanied by a hint of smoke—but he knew immediately the smoke was from himself. He should have showered.

But that wasn't the real problem.

Fuck.

Emily.

It only took him a moment to remember the events of the night before.

Emily showing up at his door. The fire. Rescuing the kitten. Emily coming back to his trailer and breaking down... needing him. Wanting him. Giving in.

And now, here they were.

He needed to pull away.

One more minute.

She shifted against him, rubbing her ass against his cock, and Damian gritted his teeth.

Fuck.

His hand had just squeezed her breast when she'd shifted.

Emily moaned, shifting again, and Damian knew he needed to let go, but for some reason, he couldn't make his hand move. At least he couldn't make it move away from her breast. She looked over her shoulder, eyes only half open, and gave him a sultry smile.

"One last time?" she asked, shifting her hips backward to slide his cock up and down between her cheeks. This time, he knew she was doing it on purpose. Little brat.

Damian pinched her nipple, making her gasp and arch against him.

Yeah, that didn't actually help his situation.

Leaning forward, he nipped her ear.

"One last time."

After all, there was very little point in pulling away now. He was already wrapped around her. Once they left the bed, it would be over. No more.

Keep telling yourself that, a little voice whispered through his mind. Damian ignored it.

That was for future Damian to deal with.

Reaching down, he lifted her leg, holding her open as he began to pepper kisses down the back of her neck and over her shoulder. Shifting his hips, he could feel the slick heat of her pussy on the tip of his dick—she was already wet and ready for him.

Last night, he'd taken his time. This morning, he wanted it fast and hard and hot. Holding her leg up, he rocked his hips, rubbing his cock between the wet folds of her pussy before lining the tip up with her entrance. Emily moaned, rocking back against him, the curves of her ass plush against his groin.

Damian thrust, sinking inside of her easily, and she whimpered in response. This position, so different from last night's, would give her entirely new sensations. It also allowed him to reach down to caress her swollen clit, teasing the little nub as he began to rock in and out of her from behind.

"Oh, yes... Daddy..."

Fuck he loved hearing her call him that. He didn't think he'd ever get tired of it.

Except this is the last time, remember? Unless...

He pushed the voice away again. It was the last time. Which meant he'd just have to enjoy it while it lasted.

Biting down on the back of her shoulder, he sucked on the skin hard enough to leave a mark. It would be easily covered by any shirt, but he'd know it was there for a few days at least. A small mark to remember him by.

"Fuck, you feel so good," he muttered against her shoulder, groaning as he kept thrusting into her at a steadily increasing pace. She whimpered, clenching around him as his fingers circled her clit, teasing her, taking her higher. "Good girl."

The shrill ring of his phone cut through the air.

Not just any ring.

Katrina's ring.

"Fuck."

Emily froze against him.

"Give me a second. I'll turn it off." There was no way he could keep fucking Katrina's best friend while his daughter's ringtone kept blaring.

The phone was on the other side of the bed, Emily's side. Still lodged deep in her pussy, Damian rolled forward. His heart rate had kicked up with the reminder that this was definitely something he *should not be doing*. He could already feel his erection threatening to deflate, despite the fact he was buried in Emily's pussy.

Now on all fours in front of him, ass in the air, Emily buried her face in the pillows while Damian fumbled for his phone with one hand, trying to keep his balance. He just needed to hit the button to reject the call…

But his finger slid against the screen when he lost his balance a bit, in exactly the wrong spot. He knew what was happening, yet he couldn't stop it.

He could only watch in horror as his daughter's face suddenly popped up on the screen.

Video call.

She'd done a video call.

You fucking idiot.

"Hi Da— DAD! OH MY GOD! WHAT ARE YOU DOING? WHO IS THAT?" Katrina's voice went from normal to screaming in less than two seconds, obliterating any hope he'd had of hiding what was going on.

Emily lifted her head in horror.

"Katrina?!" Her voice, unnaturally shrill, didn't keep his daughter from recognizing her.

"*EMILY*?!"

Fuck!

"I have to call you back!" The words came out strangled, but at least he got them out before finally grabbing the phone. He fumbled it only a little before he managed to get it turned off.

Emily easily rolled away from him since his dick was no longer inside her. It had shrunk faster than if he'd put it in an ice bath. She scrambled up against the headboard, face pale, eyes wide, looking at him in horror. He stared back at her for a long moment, the silence hanging heavy between them.

His phone started to ring again.

Katrina's ringtone.

"Fuck." He groaned. He wasn't ready to deal with this, yet he didn't have a choice. All because he'd accidentally swiped to answer instead of rejecting the call. Fucking smartphones. This would never have happened twenty years ago. Sometimes, he really missed his flip phone. Meeting Emily's miserable gaze, he sighed.

"It's not your fault. Go get dressed. I'll talk to her." He had no idea what he was going to say, but he knew he couldn't avoid it.

Emily scrambled out of his bed without a word. He waited until she was out the door, closing it behind her, to answer the phone.

This time, Katrina hadn't used the video feature, which was probably for the best since he still wasn't dressed, though at least Emily was no longer in his bed.

Fucking hell.

"Hi, sweetheart."

"Don't you 'hi, sweetheart' me! What the hell, Dad?"

Katrina was no longer shouting, but her voice was about two octaves higher than normal and shrill enough to make his ears hurt. Grimacing, he held the phone away from his head.

"Did I or did I not just see you... *doing* my best friend?"

"I don't think that's any of your business." Shit, wrong thing to say.

"Not my... *not my business?* She's my best friend! You're my dad! I am the intersection of these two things!"

"I... we didn't mean for it to happen."

"Oh, her trailer burned down, and you just accidentally fell on top of her while you were both naked? What the hell, Dad?"

"How did you know her trailer burned down?" He hadn't called her, and he was ninety-nine percent sure Emily hadn't either.

Katrina scoffed, some normality returning to her voice with the conversation. She sounded like she was calming down a little.

"You seriously think news like that wouldn't travel? I called her because I heard about the fire and that she ended up at our place. Since she wasn't answering her phone, I called *you*. I just didn't expect..."

"Right. Well..." Damian rubbed the center of his forehead. "I'm sorry you saw that. I definitely did not intend for you to."

"Oh, so you were just going to hide it from me? How is that better?"

Fortunately, he didn't have to answer that question because Emily barged back into the room without knocking.

"Let me talk to her," Emily demanded breathlessly.

Well, it wasn't like he was doing a particularly good job of it. Maybe the girls would do better. And, at the very least, he could get dressed. Wordlessly, he handed the phone off to her and hoped he was making the right choice. Taking the phone, Emily spun back around and walked into the hallway, closing the door behind her.

Damian sighed. He needed to get dressed before he talked to his daughter again.

EMILY

"What the *hell*, Emily?"

"I'm sorry, I'm sorry, I'm so sorry," Emily blurted out.

"I don't understand how this happened! You were a freaking virgin until two weeks ago! You're not the type to..."

Katrina's voice trailed off, and Emily's heart sank. Her friend knew her too well. This was exactly the line of thinking Emily had wanted to divert her from, but it was too late.

"Oh my God... Oh. My. God. When we talked about it, were you talking about... Did my *dad*—" She cut off, making a retching sound. "I think I just threw up in my mouth a little."

"I'm so, so sorry," Emily said again, wincing. "You weren't supposed to ever know."

"I can't decide whether or not that makes it better," Katrina muttered.

Phoenix looked up from where he was sitting on the kitchen table and meowed at her. Maybe it was her imagination, but it sounded a little judgmental. Sighing, she went to scratch his head before replenishing his water. She needed to go get him some food.

She hadn't even thought to check on her car last night. She was so used to not having one, she hadn't given it a second thought. At least she knew her dad hadn't torched it too; *that* she would have noticed.

"Okay, so you and my dad did the nasty. And I do mean the nasty." Katrina took a deep breath. "I'm not calling you mommy."

"Oh my God, it's not like that! It's... I don't know. It was a one-time thing."

"Are you serious? Do you hear yourself? It's already been a two-time thing! Unless... were there more times? I thought I was going to have to lecture my dad about taking advantage of you during an obviously vulnerable time, but now I'm thinking maybe you need a talking to about using my dad for his... Oh my God, I can't even say it."

Her voice was going a little shrill again, and Emily knew the joking was to get around her uncomfortable emotions. Katrina dealt with most things with dark humor. That wasn't going to cut it in this case. They needed to really talk.

"Are you mad?" Emily asked softly.

"I... I don't know what I am." Katrina sighed. "I think... I think I need to think. It would help if I knew what your intentions are toward my dad. And what his are to you."

"We said one night that first night." Emily's lips quirked up in a half-smile as Katrina made another retching sound. Unlike before, she could tell her friend was just milking it now. Well, mostly. There was probably some real feeling behind it as well. "And again last night. I just… I was really upset. My dad set the fire."

Silence.

Emily bit her lip, waiting for Katrina to say something. Phoenix meowed again, trotting up to her and demanding attention, so she reached out to scratch behind his ears, and he batted at her hand playfully. She tensed because she didn't know why her friend had suddenly gone silent. Did she not believe Emily?

"Well, dammit, how am I supposed to stay mad at you after that?" Katrina huffed. "Your dad? That fucking shit stain. What the hell?"

Relieved to change the topic, at least a little, Emily sat down as she started to relay the events of the previous evening, hoping this morning hadn't irrevocably changed their friendship forever.

21

UNCOMFORTABLE DISCUSSIONS

DAMIAN

Coming out of his room, fully dressed now, Damian was relieved to see Emily sitting in the main room of the trailer, not crying. He took that as an indication the conversation with Katrina hadn't gone terribly, at least. The phone was on the table in front of her, and the kitten was sitting on her lap.

Looking up, Emily gave him a weak smile. "She's going to call back later."

"Okay." He ran his hand through his hair and cleared his throat. "So, uh, we need to go get Phoenix some new food. And supplies. I figured I could take you out to breakfast while we do that. We should pick up clothes for you, too."

Emily blinked, as though she was trying to figure out the meaning of his words, which he'd thought were pretty clear. Then she frowned. "Don't you have to work?"

"No. I'm going to call in." Striding forward, he picked up his phone, which brought him right next to her chair. His awareness of her presence kicked up another notch, his dick twitching as if to remind him that they hadn't finished their morning interlude. Apparently, his daughter only provided a dampening effect when she was actually present in some manner. Now that she was no longer on the phone, his body was back in business. Which sucked.

"The fire chief said they'd be back to look over the trailer today in the light, and I want to talk to them about it. Plus, you'll need to file a police report, and I'm going to be there with you through that, too."

She looked as if she were about to protest, but as soon as he mentioned the police report, she snapped her mouth shut. No, she likely wouldn't want to do that on her own. She'd had her fill of cops when her mom had been arrested. And there was no way Damian was letting her go on her own. They weren't all bad, but they sure as hell weren't all good, and the 'not bad' ones had the bad habit of not intervening when the shitty ones were shitty. It was something he'd gotten into multiple fights with his cop twin about.

If Desmond was still on the force, Damian would have had no hesitation about sending Emily to him, but he wasn't. So, Damian would be there for her and make sure no one gave her any grief.

"Right." Emily took a deep breath. "So, um, breakfast and cat supplies first?"

"Sounds like a plan." The fire chief had said they'd be by midmorning, so that should give him enough time to get Emily and Phoenix situated. An officer was supposed to be coming with him.

They left Phoenix there, mewing unhappily at being left behind. Damian closed the door firmly in the cat's face and hoped the kitten didn't retaliate by shredding his furniture.

The rest of the day flew by. He didn't get any calls from work, which was good because he had his hands full with getting Emily settled in and taking care of the trailer. The cop who came by with the fire chief was respectful and sympathetic. He took the full report from her about her father's assault on her and agreed with their suspicions about him being behind the arson.

If Don was counting on an insurance payout, he wasn't going to get it.

Unfortunately, they hadn't been able to salvage

much from the trailer. A few pictures, thankfully, but none of Emily's clothes or anything fabric. They hadn't burned, but the scent of smoke clung heavily to them. Smoke had also damaged all the furniture, including everything she'd gotten for Phoenix.

Damian had assumed that would be the case and made sure they'd gotten a duplicate of everything he'd need when they got his food. Emily had protested, but Damian had pointed out that if she did need replacements, that would be another trip. She'd tried to protest when he'd paid as well, but he'd hushed her and given her a little slap on her ass, and she'd caved like the good little girl she was deep inside.

Of course, it didn't really help either of them. She kept shooting him sidelong glances, and his palm kept itching to swat her again. Katrina knowing, even if she'd freaked out, had somehow taken some of the pressure off. Maybe because the worst had already happened.

But the fact was, Katrina did know, and he needed to talk to her.

In the afternoon, Emily went out to buy herself some more clothes. Reluctantly, Damian let her go on her own, mostly because that gave him some privacy to call his daughter.

"Hi." It wasn't her normal enthusiastic greeting, but at least she'd picked up the phone.

"Hey, honey." Damian took a deep breath. "I wanted to apologize for this morning. You shouldn't have had to see that."

"No, I shouldn't have." She huffed. "I'm pretty sure you shouldn't have been *doing* that."

Damian fell silent, trying to find the right words to explain to his daughter exactly how everything had happened. What Emily meant to him.

Barring that, if he could find a way to tell her that it meant nothing and it would never happen again, and it didn't have to change anything. But he couldn't make himself say that, either. It wasn't what he really wanted.

After a long moment, Katrina sighed. "It's not really my business. I know it's not. I want you to be happy. I want Emily to be happy. I just never really saw the two of you being happy together." She made a little retching noise, and Damian grimaced.

"It doesn't... it's not like we're getting married or anything."

To his surprise, Katrina snorted.

"Please, Dad. You are the two people I know best in the world. This morning would have never happened if you two didn't mean something to each other." She sighed. "Which makes it really, really hard for me."

"I'm sorry, sweetheart." He took a deep breath.

Might as well tell the truth because Katrina did know him too well. She was right. He would never have done anything with Emily if it didn't mean something to him because he would never have risked his relationship with his daughter if it meant nothing. "Yes, I have an... interest, but that doesn't mean I'm going to pursue it."

"So you're going to take my best friend's virginity and then dump her?" It was clear what Katrina thought of that.

Damian groaned. "That isn't exactly how I'd put it..."

"That's what it boils down to, right?"

Damian pinched the bridge of his nose. Even as a five-year-old, Katrina's logic would often cut through people's bullshit, including his. He shouldn't be surprised that twenty years later, she'd be doing the same thing. "I think that's between Emily and me. I don't want you to feel like you are not a priority to me, but my private life has to be mine to run."

"You're saying I'm not the reason you won't pursue anything with Emily?"

"You're part of the reason but not the whole reason. I'm too old for her..." His voice trailed off. Okay, those might be the only two reasons.

"Pretty sure she should get to make that call for herself," Katrina responded, amusement laced through her tone. Was... was she actually advocating for him to pursue Emily?

"You would support that?" That was not at all what he'd expected. Especially after this morning. At best, he'd thought Katrina would hopefully forgive them, and everyone would do their best to forget anything ever happened.

Support had been the last thing on his mind.

"I am really uncomfortable; I'm not going to lie. Normally, I would want to talk to Emily about all sorts of... stuff. Stuff I absolutely do not want to hear about my dad." She made that little retching sound again.

Damian rolled his eyes—Katrina tended toward the dramatic—but it also made the edges of his lips curl up. If she was being dramatic, she wasn't actually upset.

"The age gap thing doesn't bother me, though. In fact, this might be a good time to tell you that I've been seeing someone."

Oh, he did not like that segue. He did not like that segue at all. On the other hand, he knew what a massive fucking hypocrite it would make him if he objected to her dating an older man.

"Mmm hmm." He tried to sound as noncommittal as he could.

"He's a bit older, but only fifteen years older than

me. He was my professor last semester." The second sentence came out in a rush, and Damian found himself pinching the bridge of his nose again. Katrina kept talking over his low groan. "He's really great, but I haven't felt comfortable talking about him because it's kind of new, and I wanted to make sure it was going somewhere before I had to deal with any judgment... but well, now, I'm not so worried about that."

Damian would be a massive fucking hypocrite, considering the age gap between Katrina and her former professor was less than him and Emily. Fuck, his head hurt.

"You didn't start dating until he was a *former* professor, right?"

"Yup. Trust me, neither of us wanted to risk the bullshit that could follow me for that." Katrina still sounded amused, but there was an edge to her voice as well, almost as if she was daring him to disapprove.

When it came to relationship disapproval, she definitely held the trump card.

Fuck.

He should just be grateful she was taking everything so well and that she wasn't freaking out and screaming at him or ending her friendship with Emily. The last thing he wanted to do was break up their relationship.

"Right, well, great. That's great. I can't wait to

meet him." He sounded completely insincere, but he was trying, and that had to count for something.

Katrina snickered, obviously amused by his lackluster attempt at enthusiasm. "I don't think we're there yet, but if we get there, I'll let you know." She paused. "Huh. I'm not sure whether I should threaten you or Emily about not hurting the other person. I guess just... you both better treat each other well, even if you don't work out."

"I will. No matter what happens with Emily and me, I do not want it to affect your friendship with her."

"That's cute, Dad, but it's always going to affect it some. It's impossible for it not to, but I think I can deal with it. Mostly. And I think I'm even rooting for you two. Mostly." She took a deep breath. "It's going to take me a while to wrap my head around it, but the more I've thought about it today, the more I've realized that at the end of the day, I just want you both to be happy. If you make each other happy, then hooray. I think."

The ambivalence wasn't at all like Katrina, but he understood why she was struggling with offering whole-hearted support.

The truth was, he wasn't sure what was going to happen with Emily. They hadn't talked about it. In fact, they'd studiously avoided talking about it during breakfast and while they were shopping.

Knowing how Katrina felt made things a little easier. Now, there was an option he didn't think would have been there before. But it all really came down to how Emily felt.

It was one thing to spend a night together; it was another to try for a relationship, especially given all their history—his friendship with her dad, hers with his daughter, and the fact that he was so much older than her. She might not want to date someone who was *literally* old enough to be her dad.

"Well, let's not put the cart before the horse," he replied, probably proving he was too old to be dating someone Emily's age, but that's what it was. "I don't know what Emily and I are going to do. We still have to talk."

"Right, well. Good luck. I guess let me know how it goes?"

"Of course."

Now, he just had to talk to Emily.

22

IS IT A DATE?

EMILY

"So… is this a date?"

"Do you want it to be a date?" Damian asked.

It still felt weird thinking of him as Damian, but after last night and this morning, 'Mr. Elliott' didn't feel right anymore, and she couldn't call him Daddy.

Shouldn't call him Daddy.

Damian it was.

"Do *you* want it to be a date?" she countered. Truthfully, she didn't know how she felt.

She'd had a brief talk with Katrina before Damian had knocked on her door and declared he was taking her out to dinner, and her bestie had been oddly supportive. Emily didn't know if she'd be as supportive if it was her dad… but on the other hand, her dad sucked. Still, if she had a good dad, she wasn't sure how she would feel.

Katrina did confess that a lot of her understanding came from her current relationship. She was dating a man who was over a decade older than her, and she hadn't told Emily because she'd been worried about being judged, especially since he was her former professor.

It wasn't as if Emily had any room to judge now.

Before Damian could answer, their food arrived at the table, and both of them went silent while their plates were put down. Emily picked up her fork and knife to start cutting her chicken while she waited for him to answer.

If he was going to answer.

Damian cleared his throat. "I… I haven't dated in a very long time. Before today, I didn't really believe that was an option. But I talked to Katrina and…" His voice trailed off.

One side of Emily's lips curved upward. "And she was oddly okay with everything? Yeah, it made me feel like maybe…" Her turn for her voice to trail off.

This was somehow just as difficult as putting her virginity up for auction. Maybe even more so. Being vulnerable physically somehow wasn't as scary as being vulnerable emotionally. She'd spent most of her life protecting herself from being hurt by her father's actions and words, from the pain of being separated from her mother after she was arrested, and the thought of taking down any of those walls was terrifying.

"I know it sounds crazy, but yes, I would like this to be a date."

Unlike her, Damian didn't have any trouble meeting her gaze as he very firmly stated his wishes. Sure, it had taken him a bit to get there, but she felt like it was more because he'd been trying to figure out how she felt and how to phrase everything. Not like her, who was just trying to figure out how to avoid rejection in case she was misreading signals.

I'm such a wuss.

"Okay. I'd like that, too." She smiled shyly at him.

"If you'd like, there's a place I'd like to take you after this date." He lowered his voice. "Somewhere we could... play if you wanted to."

"Wait, like a club?" Emily clapped her hand over her mouth as the words came out much louder than she'd intended, looking around to see if anyone had overheard her. No one was looking at her.

Right.

She hadn't said what kind of club she suspected.

"Yes, the club that runs the... event we did." Unlike her, Damian kept his tone normal, but he was keeping the same close watch on his choice of words as she was.

"Oh... I'm not sure I realized it was run through a club."

Damian frowned, lowering his hands on either side of his plate, the silverware gently clinking against the glass.

"How did you find out about the event?"

"Oh, um... heard about it when I was applying for jobs. So, it's run through a club? I've always wanted to go to one. I've read about them." She would have never known how to go about finding one, though.

Somehow, it didn't surprise her that Damian knew about it. She hadn't thought to ask how he'd found the auction. Now she had her answer.

"You can come as my guest. And meet my brother."

"Your brother?" Emily blinked in surprise. Even though she'd grown up with Katrina as her best friend, she'd never actually seen either of Damian's brothers, though she knew they existed because Katrina would sometimes reference her uncles in passing. It didn't seem like the family was very close, though.

"He runs the club."

Wow. Okay. Well, no wonder Damian had known how to find it.

"I… yes. I would like that. Did you mean for… tonight?" It had been a bit of a long day, and she'd been looking forward to going to bed early. Resting. Recovering. Wrapping her head around everything.

"Let's go tomorrow," he said, easily switching gears. That sounded better.

"What do I wear?"

"Whatever you want."

Emily rolled her eyes. That wasn't a real answer. "What do most people wear? Most of the women?"

"Anything from street clothes to leather to lace to latex." He smiled at her, his eyes dancing with amusement. "It really is whatever you're most comfortable in. No matter what you're wearing, I'll be planning on stripping it off you, anyway."

Heat flushed her cheeks, and she glanced at the tables around them again. Thankfully, he'd dropped the volume of his voice, and it didn't appear anyone had heard him, but still. "Shh," she whispered, much to his obvious amusement.

He chuckled.

Now that they'd gotten all the harder topics out of the way, the rest of dinner went much easier, with conversation flowing naturally. They didn't eat dessert at the restaurant. Instead, Daddy had her for dessert that night. Emily fell asleep in his arms, and it wasn't until the next day that she started to stress about going to the club and meeting his brother.

He went off to work, leaving her to her own devices with strict instructions to notify him immediately if she saw her father and also to take the day to relax. It had finally occurred to her that she could wear the lingerie she'd worn the night he'd taken her virginity to the club, though she did run out to the store to pick up a light coat to go over it. With the coat's hem hanging to her knees, no one would know how little she was wearing underneath.

The other stop she made was to visit her mom. As hard as it was, her mom needed to know about her dad. They'd never been able to get officially divorced since her dad had dipped out when her mom had gone to jail, and the logistics of securing a divorce had just been too difficult, but she knew that her mom considered their marriage over. After Emily updated her, her mom cursed a blue streak, then apologized, tears in her eyes, for not being able to be there for her.

Stressing that it wasn't her fault, Emily picked up her mom's spirits by telling her about the new job... then finally confessing she was dating Damian. She wasn't actually sure how the latter was going to go over, but she didn't feel right keeping it from her mom.

Though her mom was clearly a little weirded out, she didn't say so. She had a rather pinched expression, as though she was holding back her concerns by sheer force of will, which Emily appreciated. And she repeated the same line that Katrina had—*as long as you're happy*.

Which she was.

She was really, really happy. Though also scared she hadn't seen the last of her dad. After Damian told her he thought her dad was after insurance money... ugh. Not that she'd really expected her dad to care about her possessions, but it still infuriated her.

By the time Damian got home, she was all jazzed up with the anticipation of going to the BDE club. She'd put on the lingerie, and when he walked in the door, his eyes lit up the moment he saw her. She'd positioned herself carefully so he would see her as soon as he walked in, her feet beveled like the way she'd learned in high school theater to jut out one hip and make her legs look extra-long. Her hair fell around her like a cloud, and she thought she'd done a sexy job on her makeup.

"Fuck..." He uttered the curse in a hoarse voice as he came to a halt, drinking her in with his gaze. "Are you trying to kill me?"

"Definitely not," she replied tartly, shaking her head. "What good would that do me?"

Chuckling, he came forward, which was when she noticed the plastic bag he was holding in his hand. He was wearing jeans and his work t-shirt but still looked sexy as hell. She couldn't wait to see what he was going to wear to BDE tonight. Leather, she hoped.

"I've got a present for you. One more thing for tonight."

"Oh?" Emily perked up, dropping her sexy pose and holding out her hands in a 'gimme' stance, but he didn't hand the bag to her.

"I have to wash it first."

"What?" She blinked, coming to a halt.

A slow smile spread across his lips.

"I have to wash it first."

Coming forward, he moved the bag, so it was behind him, out of her reach, as he pulled her against him with one arm so he could take her lips in a hard kiss. Emily softened against him, meeting his tongue with hers, her body thrumming with anticipation as her mind raced, trying to figure out what he could mean. When he pulled away, she stared up at him, hoping he would explain.

"I'll be right back." He shifted her around, so he could go to the bathroom.

What on earth?

Curious, Emily crept forward and put her ear to

the bathroom door. She could hear the sound of plastic being opened, then some softer noises that were hard to interpret. A spray of something? What was he spraying? Hair spray? Then water running. She frowned. What could it possibly be?

When he opened the door, she nearly fell through it and ended up stumbling right into his chest. She looked up and smiled as he raised his eyebrows at her.

"Oops."

"Uh-huh."

"What? I want to know what my present is!" She widened her eyes as she looked up at him.

"Good. I'm happy to show you."

A few minutes later, she was over his lap, the skirt of her lingerie flipped up to expose her bottom, while he sat on the couch and caressed her buttocks.

"This was not what I had in mind," she grumbled. Though she was now pretty sure she knew what her present was, even though she still hadn't actually *seen* it. She couldn't decide if it really qualified as a present or not. She was as nervous about it as she was excited.

It always turned her on to read about butt stuff, but it wasn't as though she had any actual experience. She'd never had the money to buy a toy to explore, and using her own finger had just felt weird... plus, no lube.

"Trust me, you're going to enjoy this." From caressing her bottom, his fingers dipped down between her cheeks, the tips brushing over her anus, and she automatically clenched. "Just relax, Sunshine. Enjoy Daddy's present."

Taking a deep breath, Emily did her best. It helped that he called himself Daddy, as if flipping a switch inside her. Daddy shifted, and she heard the rustle of him doing... something. Then something cold and slick pushed at the wrinkled opening of her bottom just as the fingers from his other hand began to play with her pussy.

She moaned as he stroked her sensitive folds, teasing her while simultaneously pushing into her virgin bottom with his so-called 'present.' She didn't know how big the plug was, but it certainly felt bigger than his finger... bigger and harder, with considerably less give. It stretched her, making the little ring ache as it was opened wider and wider.

Whimpering, she squirmed on his lap, her pussy clenching, which made her other muscles clench as well, forcing the plug back out. Inexorably, it pushed back in, stretching her all over again, and she moaned at the sensation as Daddy began to move it back and forth inside her, pushing it a little deeper each time while also toying with her clit.

"Oh, Daddy... it's too big," she protested, her

breath catching as he pushed it deeper, shuddering from the sensation.

"No, it's not, and bigger things will be there soon enough."

Emily moaned again at the promise, her pussy tingling at the idea that he would eventually fuck her there. It was going to hurt, but part of her wanted it.

"Your safe word is 'red,' Sunshine," he reminded her.

She didn't want to say it. Part of her liked hearing Daddy deny her when she whined.

The plug pushed in, and she cried out as she was stretched over the widest part, then it was nestled inside her, her tight ring snapping shut around the thinner base and holding it still.

"Perfect. Such a pretty little plugged bottom." Daddy twisted the plug, stimulating all the little nerve endings around her entrance, and she whined again, bucking on his lap.

She felt so odd with the plug inside her, taking up so much space. It felt as though she couldn't even breathe the same way. She knew it couldn't be *that* big, but since she hadn't seen it, in her mind, it was gargantuan.

Being filled this way had all her senses buzzing, her arousal fizzing through her like a shaken-up soda, ready to explode.

"Alright, Sunshine. Up you go. Daddy needs to get ready so we can go out."

"But..." Her voice trailed off. He'd gotten her all wound up, and now he wasn't going to get her off? How rude!

Daddy chuckled, giving her pussy a little pat, as if he could read her mind. "No playing with yourself, either. You can cum when Daddy tells you to."

She pouted as she got to her feet, but she was more turned on than she'd ever been in her life.

23

PLUGGED IN THE CLUB

DAMIAN

The cute little mincing steps Emily was taking into the BDE Club entrance made Damian grin. The plug he'd inserted was on the small side, but no one would know that from the way she acted. He could imagine her muscles clenching constantly to keep it inside her, which would have the happy side effect of increasing her arousal. It was a special kind of torment. Though he'd thought about adding some nipple jewelry, he liked that—at least for a little bit—all of her focus was going to be on the way the plug felt inside her.

Since he was part owner, he didn't need to check in when he came in. He waved to Vivian, the submissive working the front desk. She'd changed her hair again, from purple to green, though she still had the shaved undercut, which he could see because she'd styled it so the rest of her hair flipped over her head and down the other side. It looked good on her. She beamed at both him and Emily, her gaze snapping back and forth between them, and he was sure her fingers were itching to pick up a phone and start spreading the gossip that Master Damian had just walked in with a woman. A much younger woman.

He'd known walking in that he was opening a big can of worms, and he'd accepted that. He wanted her to be part of his world. And he wanted Braden to know what was going on. Eventually, it would get back to Desmond, and if he could secure Braden's support for the relationship before it did, everything would be easier.

"Oh, wow," Emily breathed as Damian led her towards the door and Master James, who was doing his turn at playing bouncer, and into the club. Master James looked as intrigued as Vivian had. Keeping his hand on Emily's lower back, Damian pushed her past and into the club. Even before the door closed behind him, he could hear the explosion of noise from Vivian as she squealed loudly, and he sighed.

Still. Emily was worth it.

Glancing down at her, he smiled at her wide eyes and parted lips as she took in the club for the first time. The entrance let out on the lower level, which was lit up with red and purple lights. At the very back of the space was a well-stocked bar, though there were rules about how much one could drink if they planned on scening. Some patrons did come just to enjoy the company of fellow kinksters at the bar, though, and they could settle in and even order some food if they were so inclined, though they'd need to make their way up the curling, wrought-iron staircase to have a meal.

Red-lit booths, each with its own candelabra chandelier, lined the second floor, overlooking the balcony, which was easy to see through as it was the same black iron design as the staircase. It gave the room a very gothic vibe, the red lighting turning it a little sinister... in a fun way.

At least, in his opinion.

Emily leaned against him, snuggling up to his side, and he slid his hand up from her back to around her shoulders. Seeing her wonder and looking around the club, it was like seeing it with new eyes. It didn't hurt that he'd been away for so long.

There were some familiar faces but mostly faces he didn't know. Seeing Vivian and James in the front had given him a bit of false assurance that every-thing would be the same walking in, but it was more like visiting a school he used to go to. The building was still the same, but a lot of the people weren't.

"Do you want to look around?" he asked Emily in a low murmur she'd be able to hear despite the throbbing bass being pumped in through the sound system.

She nodded, her head turning this way and that as she took in everything.

There were several scenes already going on at the various stations around the room, and quite a few people were watching from above. Everyone was in different stages of dress—or undress—and wearing everything from electrical tape to a full-on suit. He had pulled out his old leathers, pants and vest, and Emily's eyes had lit up the moment she'd seen him, which had made him feel damn good.

She made him feel young again.

Guiding her across the floor, Damian headed toward what looked like a flogging scene. A good, gentle way to get her started. Before they reached their destination, a familiar face popped out of the crowd in front of him, beaming.

"Daddy Damian!" Shane grinned at him, his gaze flickering back and forth between Damian and Emily. Some things about the club had not changed, and Shane was one of them. Dressed in a pair of silvery latex shorts to showcase his perfect manscaping with his shoulder-length blond hair swept back in a man bun, he looked like he'd just come from performing in the *Rocky Horror Picture Show*. In one hand, he held a small bag of something unidentifiable, but Damian had his suspicions. "It's been forever! What are you doing here? And who is this delightful darling?"

Switching his beaming gaze from Damian to Emily, Shane winked with outrageous exaggeration at her, and Emily giggled. As usual, Shane's charm worked its magic, and he could feel Emily relaxing.

"This is Emily, and it's her first time to a club," Damian said. "Emily, this is Shane, submissive brat extraordinaire."

"Oh, this is the *best* club," Shane replied, his eyes lighting up with glee. "Do you want some candy corn?" He held out the bag in his hand, confirming Damian's suspicions. It would be a cold day in hell the day Shane went anywhere without candy corn. Damian had a feeling he bought in bulk.

"Yes, please." Apparently unfazed by Shane's unique conversational style, Emily shyly reached out to take some candy while Damian barely managed to keep a neutral expression on his face. Candy corn was just sweet wax. And not the fun kind that could be melted and dripped on someone.

"It's so nice to meet you. Especially since you're here with one of our OG BDEs." Shane chuckled, fluttering his eyelashes at Damian.

"What's an OG BDE?" Emily asked, not seeing the warning glare Damian was giving Shane.

"Nothing." Damian glared harder. Unfortunately, Shane was a massive brat, so Damian's glare just bounced off him like a rubber ball against cement.

"The Original Big Daddy Energy boys. Or Big Dick Energy. But since he and his brothers are all Daddies..." Shane winked again, and Damian groaned.

"The club is named after Braden," Damian argued. "Braden Dominic Elliott." Technically, it was also named after him and Desmond, but Damian didn't go by his first name of Blake, and Desmond didn't go by Bryce, so no one knew that.

They hadn't realized when they'd created the club that the initials would turn into a completely different acronym, but someone had picked up on it the first week the club was open, and it was all over after that. Braden refused to change the name, finding it funny, and once Damian realized it got under Desmond's skin, it stopped bothering him as much. Yeah, he was petty like that.

"Well, speaking of Big Bad Daddy B, he'd like to talk to you. I can keep Miss Emily company down here if you want." Shane eyed Damian, obviously waiting to see what he would do.

"She comes with me," Damian growled, despite

knowing he was playing right into Shane's hands. It seemed that Shane's title as the Gossip Queen of BDE was still firmly in place. He wouldn't be at all surprised if Vivian had been the one to send him to find out more information.

"Of course." Shane beamed, popping another piece of candy corn in his mouth. "See you after!" He gave them a little wave before disappearing into the crowd.

Damian sighed and looked down at Emily. "Change of plans. Let's go see my brother."

EMILY

Oh my God, his brother!

Somehow, the dots hadn't connected in her head right away. Granted, there were a lot of distractions going on around her that made it really hard to focus.

"I can't see your brother like this!" she squeaked, tugging at the hem of her lingerie, which just made it even more lowcut. Pulling it back up shortened the skirt to indecent heights. There was no winning.

Daddy glanced down at her. "Why not, Sunshine? You look gorgeous."

"I'm..." She was about to say she was half-naked,

but she was actually considerably more clothed than the majority of the people in the room with them. Still, though. It was Katrina's uncle!

And you're banging Katrina's dad. What's your point?

This was not the impression she imagined making on his family. On the other hand, if the club was named after his brother, then his brother was in the lifestyle, so he shouldn't judge, right?

It still felt really weird to be going to meet his brother while she was basically wearing a slip. Her butt clenched.

Wearing a slip and a plug in her ass.

Could there be a worse time for an introduction?

She didn't want to stay down on the main floor, though, not without Daddy, even though Shane had been really nice. She didn't actually know him, and she didn't want to be in a strange kink club with someone she'd just met.

When she wasn't able to come up with a real answer, Daddy smiled down at her.

"It will be fine. He's going to love you, though he's probably going to give me a hard time, so be prepared for that. Once we talk to him, we can come back down here and watch or grab a seat and watch... or find a private room where we can play a little. Whatever you want to do." Leaning down, Daddy gave her an encouraging kiss on her forehead.

Emily took a deep breath before nodding.

She could do this.

Meet Braden, then maybe watch some of the scenes, and then a private room sounded amazing. One day, she might be comfortable enough to be on display—there was something a little exciting about that thought—but she wasn't ready to jump all the way into the deep end yet.

Walking upstairs with a plug in her butt was a whole new experience. She felt as if it was going to fall out with every step she took, which made her clench, but then that made it hard to walk up the stairs, so she had to relax…

I'm never wearing a plug without underwear again.

By the time she made it to the top of the stairs, she felt like she'd run a marathon. Daddy eyed her, as if he wasn't sure why she was panting.

"Everything okay, Sunshine? If you're too nervous, we can just leave." His eyes were full of real concern.

"Oh, no, it's not that. I mean, I am anxious about meeting your brother, but it's just… the stairs… and the plug…" Her cheeks were burning hot red as she squirmed in place, embarrassment flushing through her whole body. Not that it did anything to quell her arousal. The constant clenching all the way up the stairs had made her even slicker than before, and her nipples were stiff little points rubbing against the silky fabric of her lingerie.

It didn't matter that she was about to meet his brother. She didn't think her nipples were going to chill out. Every part of her felt extra sensitive.

"Ah, yes. The plug." Something in his eyes glinted, and she shivered. She liked it when he got all dark and dangerous like that. "Too bad I didn't get a vibrating one."

"Oh, no, that's not too bad at all," she said fervently, making him chuckle.

"Something for the future. Come on." He guided her forward, heading along the balcony to a door on the far side. A large panel of black, mirrored glass made up a big section of the wall, right after where the door was, providing a view of the whole first floor for anyone who happened to look up at it. She was pretty sure it was one-way glass and guessed there were probably people inside the room looking down.

Which meant, if his brother was in there, he'd probably seen them arrive. Emily shivered again and wasn't sure if it was from apprehension or excitement. This was a whole new world she'd just stepped into, and now she had to meet Daddy's brother.

Huh... did that make him her uncle?

24

FACING THE FAMILY

EMILY

As soon as they walked through the door of the office, Daddy ground to a halt, and Emily looked around in alarm, trying to figure out why. Then she stopped and also stared because there was a Daddy double in the office, sitting on the couch next to another man, except he was... different. It wasn't just that his hair was a little neater or that he was wearing a business suit. There was something about his expression she couldn't define. She would know the difference between him and Daddy immediately, though, despite the fact they were otherwise identical.

"Bryce," Daddy growled, glaring at his double.

"Blake." Daddy Double turned his gaze to Emily,

looking her over from head to toe in a way that both disconcerted and annoyed her. He'd better not be judging her for what she was wearing just because he was in a suit. "And who is this?"

"She's mine."

Yeah, that did things to her. And made her feel a little surer of herself. She met Daddy Double's gaze. *Bryce, Daddy called him Bryce...* but he'd also called Daddy by his first name, which she knew, thanks to Katrina. She also knew that Daddy hated his first name and preferred Damian.

"Hello." The man on the couch next to Bryce waved at her with a smile. He, too, had a full head of silver hair and a neatly trimmed goatee. He was wearing a suit as well, but he was a lot friendlier. "I'm Desmond's husband, Bastian. Don't mind Desmond. He's not always like this."

Desmond. And now she was going to kick Katrina for never mentioning that her Uncle Desmond was her dad's freaking identical twin.

"Just when I'm around," Daddy said, shifting and guiding her toward the chairs on the other side of the room from the couch, which was when she noticed the final man in the room. He was sitting behind a big desk, which was clearly his, and he was the only one who had dark hair. Clearly a little younger than the others, he still had the same penetrating gaze of the other men. "Hey, Braden."

Katrina's other uncle, the youngest one, obviously.

"Damian." Braden nodded his head in greeting, still watching her with curiosity as Damian sat down in one of the chairs in front of Braden's desk before pulling her onto his lap. "And this must be Emily."

Daddy rolled his eyes.

"You know it is. I'm sure you had plenty of time to look over her paperwork when I submitted the guest application." Daddy gave her thigh a reassuring squeeze.

"Hi," she said, waving at Braden, then directing it toward Bastian and Desmond as well. It didn't hurt to be polite, even though she wasn't sure she liked Desmond or the way he was looking at her. She realized it might not be about her, though. Clearly, the twins didn't get along.

On the other hand, she didn't like being judged based on her company, especially because she was with her Daddy.

"Isn't she a little young for you?" Desmond asked disapprovingly, looking past her to meet Daddy's gaze and confirming her dislike of him.

Emily scowled. Being on Daddy's lap made her

feel braver than she might have otherwise. "Aren't you a little old to be this rude?" she retorted.

His eyebrows flew up in astonishment, and her Daddy chuckled but squeezed her thigh again. This time, it felt more like a warning... but he didn't reprimand her. It seemed as if she was allowed to brat at his twin, but he didn't want her to take it too far.

"Aren't you?" Desmond was looking at her now, and his expression was fierce enough that if she hadn't been emboldened by sitting on her Daddy's lap, she probably would have tried to hide.

"Am I too young or too old? And besides, you started it. Don't dish it out if you can't take it." She stuck out her tongue at him, and Bastian quickly turned his laugh into a cough, causing Desmond to turn and glare at him. Braden didn't bother hiding his chuckle.

"Blame Braden. He's the reason we got to this point," Daddy said genially. "If it wasn't for that auction, I would have never touched her."

Suddenly, the atmosphere in the room changed. Braden sat up straighter, no longer chuckling, a confused frown on his face, and Damian and Bastian were exchanging an equally confused look.

"Auction? What auction?" Braden asked, snapping out the question in a way that made her jump.

"The auction... the one run through BDE? To fulfill people's fantasies? The virgin auction?"

"The what?" Desmond was so outraged he leapt to his feet.

Emily scrunched in on Daddy's lap, overwhelmed by the sudden outpouring of masculine rage around her. Daddy wrapped his arms around her, holding her more securely.

"Don't look at me like that, it's fucking run through BDE. Look at Braden. I found out about it from another member. The site itself is full of our members, and I figured it was some new promotion Braden started. Are you seriously telling me it's not?" Daddy didn't even glance at his twin. He was looking directly at Braden, as if he could make Desmond disappear through sheer force of will.

"It's not. I don't know anything about it." Braden held his hands up in surrender, looking back and forth between his two older brothers. "I swear." He looked at Emily. "You aren't a member here. How did you hear about the auction?"

"Uh... oh... well..."

"I've been wondering that myself," Daddy said, shifting her around on his lap so he could see her face.

Emily blushed. Maybe she should have expected to have to tell him about it, but it hadn't come up yet... and if Katrina's reaction had been anything to go by, she had a feeling Daddy's would be even worse.

"I..." She peeked over at the others. "Can I whisper it in your ear?"

Bad enough admitting the path that had led her to the auction to him; having to talk about it—including her money troubles—in front of a bunch of men who were basically strangers was more than she could bear. Daddy's expression was blank as he nodded, as if he was very carefully trying not to give anything away. At least he realized he wasn't going to like it.

Maybe this wouldn't be so bad.

DAMIAN

He was going to hurt someone.

Unfortunately, the person he wanted to hurt the most was himself. How had he not noticed what dire straits Emily was in?

And a fucking strip club?

The auction had been risky enough, but now, knowing how she'd gotten there, he wanted to punch someone in the face.

Of course, he had an identical twin. It would almost be like punching himself in the face…

No, don't take your anger at yourself out on Desmond. He's an asshole, but he doesn't deserve that.

It really would feel good, though.

Turning his head to bury his face in her hair, he growled in her ear. "You are *never* allowed to let your situation get that bad again, do you hear me? I don't care how or why. You will come to me for help. Period."

Emily huffed in indignation, squirming away from his lips, so he could see her roll her eyes at him. "Well, of *course,* I'd come to you *now*." It wasn't her words that made her sound disrespectful; it was her 'duh' tone.

Damian raised his eyebrows at her, and she flushed. Oh, his little girl was going for a hell of a spanking after this. The danger she'd put herself in, the brattiness that was coming through now… it was one thing to brat to his twin, another to him.

He looked at his brothers. Emily clearly didn't want him spreading her business.

"It wasn't through a member of the club, but I have a feeling it was someone who knows a member. I'll track it down and let you know."

Desmond looked like he wanted to protest, but Bastian reached over to put his hand on Desmond's knee, which made him settle down, though he still looked grouchy. Then again, maybe his face had just frozen like that, the way their mother had always warned it would.

"I'm just pissed someone is running a freaking auction out of my club, and I didn't know about it." Braden was flushed, fists clenching and unclenching on the desk in front of him. He looked at Damian. "Can you show me the website?"

"Sure. Stay here, Sunshine." Damian shifted Emily off his lap, so she stayed in the chair while he went around to the other side of Braden's desk to get on his computer. It only took him a moment to pull up the website and use his password to get in. By that time, Desmond and Bastian were crowding around to see it as well.

He glanced up to see Emily curled up in the chair, watching them with wide eyes. The expression on her face was reminiscent of the one from that first night, and he felt the rush of arousal surge down to his groin. But he still needed to punish her. His hand was itching to give her a well-deserved spanking.

Yes, he'd already spanked her once before over putting her pride before her safety, but that was before he knew how bad it had been.

That was before she was *his*.

Meeting his gaze, Emily started squirming in her seat, as though she could sense his thoughts.

"What the fuck!" Braden exclaimed, drawing Damian's attention back to the computer screen. "It's almost all members. Where... what..."

"We'll help you look into this," Bastian said, putting his hand on Braden's shoulder. "Don't worry. We'll get to the bottom of it."

"Would have helped if we'd known about it sooner." Of course, Desmond was going to blame Damian.

"Well, Detective, you wouldn't have known about it at all if it wasn't for me." Damian smirked at his twin, who scowled deeper. "Excuse me for thinking that Braden was trying out a new thing for the club. It's not the worst idea in the world, and it's clearly making a lot of money. Plus, no one was coerced. Emily signed up of her own free will, and there's nothing to indicate there's anything illegal going on with the auction itself... it's just the fact it looks like it's connected to BDE."

"And a million things could go wrong with that, *Blake*."

"But they haven't yet, and we have the chance to stop it before anything does, thanks to me, *Bryce*." Damian raised his eyebrows at Desmond. "Aren't you going to thank me, bro?"

It would be a cold day in hell before his twin ever admitted that Damian had gotten one over on him.

"Play nice, you two," Bastian admonished, still watching as Braden scrolled through the various offerings on the site.

Desmond had a point that something could go terribly wrong. The site looked like it was connected to BDE, which meant anything that did go wrong would be on them, even if they hadn't known about the auction. The connection also probably made their members think it was legitimate in every way... the same way Damian had.

But it would be a cold day in hell before he ever admitted his twin was right about something.

"Actually, Bastian, while you're here, could I ask a favor?" He was glad Bastian was there because he'd been gearing himself up to reach out to Desmond, which would have been painful. Now, he could ask both of them while pretending he was only talking to his twin's partner.

"Of course, what do you need?" Bastian straightened up. Even Desmond's expression changed to something more serious. Damian never asked them for favors. Yes, he was technically only asking Bastian, but everyone knew that asking Bastian was the same as asking both of them.

He glanced at Emily before updating them on the

situation with her father. Yes, she'd filed the police report, but sometimes, it took someone behind the scenes to really get things moving. Hearing that her own father had burned up her trailer had both Bastian and Desmond scowling.

Desmond didn't even give him shit about needing a favor.

"We'll find out what's going on with the investigation," he promised before Bastian could, looking over at Emily. "And we'll find him."

"Thank you." She looked down at her hands. "I feel like a bad daughter, but..."

"He was a shit father first," Damian said, walking back around the desk to crouch down in front of her and take her hands in his. He gentled his tone. "He doesn't deserve your protection, much less deserve you as a daughter. He's lucky to have had you, and it's his loss that he doesn't know that."

She managed a tremulous smile for him. "Thanks, Daddy."

His heart swelled in his chest.

"And on that note," Desmond said behind him. "Let's give these two some privacy to talk while we go question some of the members. There are a few down on the floor who are on the site. We can start with them."

Sometimes, Damian hated how well Desmond knew him even though he was also grateful for it.

His brothers and Bastian gave Emily either a nod or a smile on their way past as Damian got to his feet, crossing his arms over his chest and staring down at her. She scrunched into the chair as if she was trying to make herself smaller.

"Little girl, you are in big trouble."

※ 25 ※

LEARNING HER LESSON

EMILY

"I didn't do anything!" Her butt automatically clenched around the plug in her bottom. She said the words, but she'd known she was in trouble from the moment she whispered her story about finding the auction in Daddy's ear. He didn't like that she'd gone to get a job at a strip club.

But it wasn't like she'd known he had money back then!

Not that she'd asked.

If she'd told Katrina how badly things were going for her, her friend would have been able to tell her. Then she wouldn't have gone to the strip club and found out about the auction and sold her virginity to

Daddy. As Daddy raised his eyebrow at her, she switched gears. "We wouldn't be together if I hadn't."

"Not a good enough reason to put yourself in danger. You don't know what would have happened if you hadn't. If you'd told Katrina or your mom the truth, both of them would have told you to come to me for help. Katrina might have wanted to do it herself, but she would have asked me, which means I would have known about it, eventually. We might have ended up here without you having to put yourself through all of that."

Well... well... poop.

She couldn't think of a good counterargument.

"I already learned my lesson the last time you spanked me," she said earnestly, pressing her thighs together.

For some reason, trying to get out of her punishment, knowing it was coming anyway, was turning her on. In fact, she'd be disappointed if Daddy didn't spank her at this point. Even though he was scowling, she could tell he wasn't truly angry-angry. He wasn't happy, but he wouldn't be too harsh, either.

And she wanted the spanking.

She craved the release.

She was all wound up inside with everything that had happened in the past few days, and it would feel so good to let it all out.

"Let's make sure of it. Stand up, Sunshine." He held out his hand for her to take.

Emily huffed but didn't argue. She didn't want to give him a *real* reason to spank her, after all. Taking his hand, she got to her feet, clenching around the plug as she did so.

Daddy guided her over to the desk and pushed some of the papers to the side, clearing a space for her right on the edge.

"Bend over."

The way he was positioning her had her looking out the big tinted window down onto the club floor. They were far back enough that she couldn't see *everything*, but she could see a good portion of the far side of the club. Someone was being whipped. Someone else was being spanked. Another someone was being tied up with ropes and lifted into the air.

Emily shivered as her body pressed against the cool, hard wood, drinking in the sights of the club. She was sure Daddy had positioned her facing this direction for exactly that reason. The flimsy skirt of her slip was flipped up and over her butt, baring it completely—not like the silky lingerie would have been much protection, but being totally naked from the waist down had a psychological effect that couldn't be denied.

"I almost forgot this pretty little bottom was

plugged right now," Daddy said, tugging on the base. Emily squealed at the sensation as her ring stretched slightly, then clenched, her automatic reflex trying to hold it inside her. He twisted it, sending a pulse of pleasure through her, her pussy spasming emptily. "Good. As soon as I'm done spanking these cheeks a nice, hot pink, Daddy's cock is going in this cute little ass."

"Oh God..." She shivered at the thought. Even though it was exactly what she wanted, it was still scary.

"No... oh, Daddy," Daddy corrected.

That was the worst Dad joke ever, and she would have said something, but his hand came down hard on her butt, and she shrieked at the sting.

"Ow!" She started to buck up, but his hand was already there, pushing her back down, flattening her breasts against the wood beneath her. It didn't deter him one bit as he kept spanking her with crisp, firm swats that made her squirm desperately between the hand holding her down and the hard desk.

The hot pain flared across her senses as pleasure pulsed through her when she clenched around the plug. The spanking felt different with the plug inside her, big and intrusive, and feeling more so as her muscles reacted to the slaps raining down on her upturned cheeks. The heat and sting were growing with every swat, making her pant and whimper—though she didn't squeal again now that she knew what to expect.

"Owie, owie, owie," she started chanting as Daddy's hand came down on already heated flesh, making her even hotter. When he moved his hand down to her sit spots, she squeaked in reaction. Those spots hurt so much more, the sting amplifying... yet when he ran his hand over her pussy, she could feel how swollen and wet she was.

"Next time you need help, are you going to ask for it?"

"Yes! I already learned that lesson!" She gripped the sides of the desk hard, panting as he stroked her wet folds, quivering from the switch in sensations from pain to pleasure. Her body was struggling to tell the two apart, the painful heat turning to a simmering stew of arousal as he played with her, teasing her.

"Just making sure to drive it home since you kept part of the story from me." He gave her pussy a little spank, not nearly as hard as he'd been spanking her butt.

She cried out at the hot sensation. The area was much more sensitive, and the stinging burn made her dance in place, her clit throbbing from the impact of his fingers.

He spanked her pussy again, and she writhed in place against the table as she panted for breath, the erotic pain rippling through her in waves.

When he gripped the base of the plug and pulled, she moaned, her muscles automatically clenching to try to keep it inside even as her excitement rose. Freshly spanked, her pussy throbbing, and in the office of a real BDSM club... losing her anal virginity here would go far beyond any of her fantasies. It was hot as hell, as well as somewhat terrifying. The plug eased out of her, leaving her feeling so very empty.

"I'm going to fill this pretty little ass and make sure you know who you belong to." Daddy's words were accompanied by another swat to her already seared cheek.

Emily squealed at the unexpected sting. She panted, holding herself in position, able to see some of him in the reflection on the glass... like a shadowy figure moving behind her, working his hand over his cock before placing the tip at her entrance.

Emily's breath caught in her throat. His tip was much bigger than the plug's. No tapering here—just a thick, hard, blunt rod pushing into her, stretching her open.

Pressing her forehead against the cool wood of the desk, she shuddered, her toes curling as Daddy's cock forced its way past the tight ring of her sphincter. The plug had gotten bigger and bigger until she'd finally gotten past the thickest part, and her ring had been able to close around the nook between the bulb and the base… but there was no nook now.

The mushroom head was as close as it got. She felt it push past her entrance, but his shaft was nearly as thick, giving her straining ring absolutely no quarter. He barely had the tip of his dick inside her, and she already felt full to the brim. She wasn't sure if he'd put some extra lube on his cock or if she was still just slick from the plug, but he had no problem pushing past her clenching muscles.

"Good girl, that's it. You feel so good around Daddy's cock." He groaned as he thrust in deeper, rocking his hips forward, his hands coming down on her hips to pin her to the desk as he slid inside her.

His words sent a tremor through her. The discomfort was nothing compared to the pleasure she knew she was giving him… in fact, it made it better.

She wanted to be held down, used, to whimper from the sting, and be ignored while Daddy took her ass hard. The pain, his dominance, was more than just physical. It danced around in her brain. Something about his cock sliding in where nothing was supposed to enter made her feel so acutely submissive, so completely helpless.

Then he rocked back, withdrawing to just the tip,

and the sensation felt like nothing she'd ever experienced. Her fingernails clawed at the desk beneath her as she writhed, her breath stuttering. It felt like a wave receding, but inside her, and there was nothing she could do about it as it drew back while she remained pinned in place.

It only lasted for a moment before he was thrusting back in, sliding deeper this time. Emily cried out as her pussy spasmed in response. The rough stretch bordered on painful, even as pleasure throbbed through her.

"Daddy, it's too big! It hurts!" She didn't mean to say the words, but they came out anyway as she struggled on the edge of pleasure and pain. Deep down, what she wanted—what she really wanted—was to be denied.

And Daddy knew it.

"Take a deep breath, Sunshine. You can take it. Your ass was meant to take Daddy's cock."

Another withdrawal left her squirming and whining under his hands, then he thrust in again, this time sliding all the way home until his body was resting against her roasted cheeks. Emily moaned, shuddering and clenching around the thick cock that was now filling her completely. She felt so full, so submissive, so... possessed.

Daddy was claiming her, exactly the way he'd

promised he would. Holding himself inside her so she could feel every inch of him, he rubbed her hot buttocks with his hand, seemingly waiting for her to adjust. Squirming, panting, Emily wasn't sure she ever would. How could she?

Then Daddy's hand moved away, and a moment later, she heard a click and a faint hum... her hips bucked upwards when he slid his hand beneath her, pressing a small but very strong vibrator against her clit.

"Daddy!" Her bottom clenched around him hard as she shuddered against the buzz of the vibrator, bucking up against him as if she could get him any deeper inside her.

"Come for me, Sunshine. Come for Daddy while he fucks your ass." He pressed the vibrator firmly against her clit as he thrust into her with hard, long, deep strokes.

Emily cried out as her senses went haywire from the overwhelming onslaught of exquisite agony.

DAMIAN

Emily broke apart beneath him as he moved, fucking her hard against his brother's desk, holding the vibrator firmly against her clit. She was so tight, he knew he wasn't going to last long. He'd wanted her to really feel the intimate invasion of his cock taking her ass for the first time, but now he wanted her to enjoy it, too... mostly.

The little finger vibrator was very powerful and could easily move from the pleasure of release to painful oversensitivity... which wasn't necessarily a bad thing. He truly wanted Emily to remember tonight's lesson.

"Daddy! Oh fuck!" She screamed out her pleasure, her ass tightening around him as he thrust, stimulating every inch of his well-lubed cock.

It was a good thing he'd added extra lube because her tight grip would have stopped him in his tracks otherwise. This way, she spasmed around him, but he was able to keep riding her hard, which he knew would send even more sensations crashing through her.

Writhing in abject ecstasy, Emily sobbed out her climax, bucking up against him as she tried to escape the relentless buzzing of the vibrator against her swollen clit.

"Daddy, please! I can't... I can't... *Daddy!*"

Her body seized, and he leaned forward, burying himself deep inside her, his cock throbbing as the tight ring of her entrance clamped down hard around the base, almost tight enough to be a cock ring. He groaned as the first spurts of his orgasm forced their way past that grip.

Her muscles worked his cock, milking him as he emptied himself into her bowels while she shuddered and panted. The sweet sobs of her sensual overload were music to his ears as he ran the finger vibe around her clit one last time. Emily screamed, shuddering and spasming, writhing beneath him, wringing the last drips of cum from his balls.

Damian groaned, barely managing to keep his knees from buckling. Leaning forward, he braced himself on his elbows against the table and flicked the vibe's off-switch. The heat from her spanked cheeks warmed his groin as his breathing slowed, and he came back to himself. Looking up, he could see down onto the floor where his brothers and Bastian were making their way through the crowd of people, pausing for conversations.

He was pissed the auction wasn't legal, wanted to take it down, yet grateful it had brought him Emily. Which was kind of fucked up, but he couldn't deny his mixed emotions. He knew he would still be pining over her if it wasn't for the auction.

"Good girl," he said, leaning down to kiss the back of her shoulder. She shuddered as he pulled away, his softening cock sliding easily from her stretched opening. "Stay right here, and don't move."

Emily murmured something that might have been 'yes, Daddy' and slumped on the desk.

He doubted she was going anywhere right now.

Braden had a full bathroom attached to the office, which was nearly as big as the office itself and fully equipped with anything a kink club owner might want if he had cause to use a full bath. Damian quickly cleaned both himself and Emily's plug off before applying a new coat of lubricant to the toy. When he walked back into the office, she was right where he'd left her, pink butt still on display, her crinkled rosebud still pouting slightly open, with a small drip of pearly cum decorating the rim. Between her slick, puffy pussy lips, her clit was pink and still swollen, likely thanks to being overstimulated by the vibrator.

"Very good girl," he said approvingly as he came up behind her. Emily sighed when he put his hand on her bottom, then whimpered as he pushed the plug back into the abused hole. "There. That'll keep Daddy's cum in your ass until we get home."

She moaned in response, shuddering a little, and Damian patted her bottom approvingly.

"You're a dirty Daddy," she accused, her voice throaty from all her moans and whimpers.

"When it comes to you, absolutely." He helped her up from the desk.

Dirty, depraved... and utterly devoted. She was utter perfection, and he was old and wise enough to know he would never be able to let her go. He was falling in love. Despite everything. Hell, he'd already fallen. All he had to do was hope she felt the same way.

RELATIONS

EMILY

"I wish I could tell you more about the club," Emily said wistfully. "It was amazing." The only downside of Damian being her Daddy was not being able to really talk to Katrina about it. She could share some things, but she'd always imagined that once she was having sex like everyone else, she'd be able to share lots of details.

Then again, Katrina had never been detailed with what she shared, but Emily had assumed that was because she didn't want to rub her sex life in Emily's face. Maybe that was just how Katrina was. Besides, she completely understood why Katrina might not want to hear about how big her dad's penis was or how well he used it.

She was very curious about BDE but also slightly horrified at knowing her uncles were not only involved there but actually owned the place.

"Tell me all you want about the club, just not anything else." Katrina made her usual gagging noise. "I still can't believe Uncle Braden is running a freaking sex club." She made the noise again.

"Well, I still can't believe you never told me that your dad had a twin, so it seems like everyone's keeping secrets."

"It just never came up!" Katrina laughed. She'd been taken aback when Emily had said something to her. Apparently, she just hadn't thought much about it, and it had never occurred to her to tell Emily that her dad had a double out there in the world. Especially since, according to Katrina, they didn't see Desmond that much except at big family holidays.

"Yeah, well..."

"Oh my God, don't you dare say 'unlike your dad's cock'!"

"I wasn't going to!" That was something Katrina would say, not Emily. She couldn't help but laugh. Of course, Katrina's head would go there. "I don't even have to make the joke. You do it to yourself!"

"And I need to stop cuz... eeeeeeeeew." Katrina went quiet for a moment. "I do love you, though. You know that, right? This is weird for me, but at the end of the day, I just want you both to be happy."

"I know. And I love that about you. And he makes me happy."

"Even though it's only been like a week."

"To be fair, it's been a really intense week. And even if we weren't dating, we... you know... several weeks ago."

"I do know and wish you hadn't given me so much detail when you first told me about it." More gagging noises.

"If I'd thought you would ever know I was talking about your dad, I wouldn't have," Emily said, defending herself. She'd figured Katrina would never know. It was supposed to be a mystery. If she'd known Katrina would eventually find out, she wouldn't have provided nearly as much detail about how good in bed her 'mystery' deflowerer had been.

But she'd wanted to tell someone, and Katrina was not only her best friend, she was probably Emily's only real friend.

That really put a lot of pressure on her not to fuck up the relationship with Katrina's dad since she didn't want to ruin her relationship with Katrina. The smart thing to do would be to pull away before it became an issue... but she'd been living in his trailer all week, sleeping in his bed, and she was in so deep, she couldn't see the exit anymore.

She didn't really want to.

It was so fast—too fast some people might say—but it felt right in every way. Even things with Katrina were a lot less awkward, other than her bestie not wanting to hear about her sexcapades… but considering she'd never really had sexcapades to talk about before, it didn't feel like a change.

"How are things going with your former professor?" Emily asked. Damian had been the one to tell her about him, not Katrina, which made her wildly curious. She'd been waiting for Katrina to bring him up, but since her bestie was apparently staying quiet about it, she decided to go ahead and ask.

"Oh, we broke up already." Katrina sounded more morose than brokenhearted. "He wasn't what I thought he was going to be. But hey, at least it helped me understand the appeal of an older man. Otherwise, I'd be a lot more freaked out about you and my dad."

"That is an upside," Emily agreed. "I'm sorry it didn't work out with him, though."

"Yeah, I'm sorry I didn't tell you about him. I thought you might judge me. Either because of the age difference or the fact he'd been my professor, or whatever, and I just didn't want to tell people about it until I thought it was really going somewhere."

"That makes sense, but I wouldn't have judged you. It's your life."

"I know. I think I was judging myself a little. I think even in the beginning, I knew he wasn't right for me." Katrina sighed. "It's just hard being single out here. Everyone just wants hookups, and no one wants a relationship."

"I'm sorry, hun, that really sucks." Emily had never really known what it was like to date, but from observation, it didn't look all that fun. She'd gone straight from selling her virginity into a relationship, all by accident, and somehow, that was a lot better than having to date. Which said a lot about the state of the dating world right now.

"Alright, enough wallowing. I've gotta go to rehearsal and rant about my angry vagina." Despite her words, Katrina sounded pretty upbeat. Whatever her feelings had been about her newest ex, she was already moving on. At least, as far as Emily could tell, though Katrina had always been good about covering her feelings post-breakup.

"Have fun. I miss you."

"I miss you, too." Katrina made a kissing noise and hung up the phone.

Sighing, Emily made her way over to the kitchen area, where Phoenix was sunning himself on the windowsill above the sink. She hadn't quite made it to him yet when his head suddenly lifted, and he jumped to his feet, all the fur along his body lifting up as he hissed. Startled, she stepped back in surprise before hurrying forward to see what he was looking at.

Her dad.

This particular window had a perfect view of the bus stop and entrance to the park, and her dad had just gotten off the bus. There was no mistaking him —not that he was trying to hide. He swaggered along the sidewalk without a care in the world.

"It's okay," she said to Phoenix, stroking her hand down his back to try to calm him. Not that it worked. "He's not getting away. Not this time."

Shooting a quick text off to Damian, she headed for the door, only pausing to grab the mace hanging from the key rack next to it.

DAMIAN

It had been a while since Damian had seen Elizabeth. Too long, really. He'd visited more often before he'd started being attracted to Emily. He hadn't visited much the past couple of years because it felt weird to visit Elizabeth when he was lusting after her daughter. He'd felt guilty.

Not that he felt less guilty now, but the imperative to visit her was greater. Especially considering what he wanted.

"So." Elizabeth tapped her fingers against the metal table in between them. She'd aged since being convicted, yet she looked healthier. Her eyes were sharp and focused, all of her attention engaged on him. "You and Emily."

"Me and Emily." He held his hands out on the table, palms up, in a gesture of surrender. "I didn't mean for it to happen."

"I know. You're not the type. Which is what makes it all the more surprising." She shook her head. "I don't really know what to say to you. I know you're a good man, but the age thing…"

"I know. If it helps, Katrina almost immediately informed me that her current boyfriend is not only her former professor but also closer to my age than hers, so I have some idea how you feel."

Elizabeth laughed, looking more like the woman he remembered.

"Ah, the trials and tribulations of being a parent." She sighed. "In the end, it's up to Emily. I am definitely not one to be judging anyone else's decisions. I ended up with Don and stayed with him for far too long."

"No one could have known how he would turn out when you married him," Damian argued. Hell, he'd been the best man at their wedding. "He wasn't like that originally. He just... changed."

"But you haven't. You were a good man from the beginning. You helped us out every step along the way." Elizabeth tilted her head back, looking up at the ceiling, as though she was searching for answers. "That's what makes this so weird."

"I know. I promise I didn't even look at Emily this way until a year or two ago. Definitely not when she was a kid or anything. I just turned around one day, and there she was. Sweet, beautiful, kind, so damn determined, and... well, for some reason she feels the attraction back."

"For some reason." Elizabeth snorted as she met his gaze again. "You've always been a handsome man, and you know it." She shook her head, a small smile playing on her lips. "When it comes down to it, what I want most is for Emily to be happy. You made Anita happy for a long time."

"I did. We were happy together. And I still miss her, but..."

"But you deserve a life." Elizabeth smiled, reaching out her hand across the table and placing it in Damian's. He closed his fingers around it, feeling the warmth of the long friendship they'd had. "You deserve to be happy. You spent so much time pouring all of your energy into Katrina. Now, she's all grown up, and you feel like you can finally be you again."

"Yes. That's it exactly." He let out a long sigh of relief that Elizabeth wasn't angry at him, even if she didn't really understand.

"I want that for you, too. And I want that for Emily." She squeezed his hand. "If you are what makes her happy, I won't stand in your way. I've caused my baby girl enough pain."

"That's really good to hear." Damian took a deep breath, his free hand reaching into his pocket to pull out a small velvet box. "Because I'm going to be asking for more than your acceptance. I was hoping to get your blessing."

He held out the box in his hand, and Elizabeth stared at it for a long moment, as if it might suddenly come to life and bite her. Releasing his hand, she picked up the box and opened it. Even though her elbows were braced on the table, he could see that her hands were trembling. Damian kept his mouth shut.

He was asking a lot of Elizabeth, and he wasn't going to push her through this critical moment.

She popped the box open and let out a low whistle.

"It was my grandmother's. It was never Anita's style, but I think it's Emily's."

"And you don't want Katrina to have it?" Elizabeth looked up from the perfect cushion cut diamond, flanked on either side by sapphires.

"Anita wanted Katrina to have her ring. It's waiting for Katrina in a safe deposit box for her engagement or her thirtieth birthday, whichever comes first."

"I see." Elizabeth looked back at the ring she was holding. "It does look perfect for Emily." She snapped the box shut. "Don't you think you're moving a little fast, though?"

"I know what I want and don't see any point in waiting." The side of his mouth quirked up. "Especially at my age."

"You're terrible." But she was laughing again, even as she shook her head and handed the box back to him. "Just make her happy, okay? That's all I want."

"That's all I want, too. I promise, Elizabeth. I'm going to take care of her."

Taking a deep breath, Elizabeth nodded her head. "Then you have my blessing."

It was the first time he'd ever walked out of the jail with a smile on his face. A smile that disappeared when his phone buzzed as he reached his motorcycle and saw the text message Emily had just sent him.

"Fuck!"

Damian threw himself onto his seat, yanking his helmet over his head, and peeled out of the parking lot as fast as he could.

❧ 27 ❧

CATCHING THE ARSONIST

EMILY

Gripping the slim canister of mace in her hand, thumb at the ready, Emily stormed out of the trailer, though she made sure to shut the door behind her. Phoenix yowled at her, but there was no way she was going to put her cat in a position where her dad might be able to hurt him again. And she would not be abandoning this trailer. Her dad wasn't going to get the opportunity to burn anything down this time.

She'd mace him first.

Two weeks ago, she wouldn't have been able to imagine doing such a thing to her own dad. That was before he tried to burn down her trailer with her cat in it.

She had a lot of pent-up rage to vent.

"Hey!" she yelled as she bounded down the steps.

Her dad had gone past the trailer, probably headed toward the wreckage of hers, and he turned in confusion.

"How *dare* you come back here after burning down my trailer?"

"*My* trailer," he corrected her, shoving his hands in his pockets and smiling at her like she'd said something funny.

Emily stormed closer to him, gripping the mace so tightly, she had to remind herself not to accidentally squeeze the trigger and set it off. She stopped about ten feet away—close enough to talk but far enough he couldn't easily reach her.

"And it was an accident... of course." His expression turned to one of false sympathy. "Did you lose anything important to you, sweetheart? Maybe if you hadn't been such a bitch, that wouldn't have happened."

Any hesitation she had about him getting his just desserts died at that moment. "I hope you don't think you're getting a payout from the insurance company or anything. The fire chief already pegged it as arson, and the cops are looking for you." She reached into her back pocket and pulled out her phone, taking another step back as she slid her finger over the screen.

The smirk on his lips was replaced by fury. "Don't you dare, you little bitch!"

He lunged for her, but Emily was ready for him this time. She swung her arm up, turning her head, and spraying him right in the face. Immediately, she backed up as he screamed, one arm coming up to cover his eyes, the other still trying to reach for her as he stumbled forward.

"My eyes! My eyes! What the fuck did you do, you stupid cunt?!" Her dad was screaming like he was dying, his hand groping for her.

Emily dodged out of the way.

"Take him down, Em!" Rio was running toward her from down the street while others were coming out to see what all the commotion was about.

Emily dodged around her dad and kicked at the back of his knee. She felt it connect, felt the shock as he went down heavily on his knees, catching himself with the hand he'd been trying to grab her with. Before he could try to get up, Rio was there, pushing her dad back down and grabbing his hands to secure them behind his neck. She gaped at him, and when Rio looked up to see her expression, he winked at her.

"Call the cops, chica," he ordered.

He was almost as bossy as her Daddy, but she immediately did as he said. Her dad wasn't getting away with anything.

Neighbors came to gather around, watching as her dad spit vitriol at Rio. The muscular man didn't seem bothered at all, perfectly happy sitting on her dad's back until the cops arrived. A car pulled up, and Damian got out— no... Emily caught herself as her heart leapt in her chest.

It wasn't her Daddy; it was her Daddy Double. Bastian and Desmond had arrived on the scene, both of them hurrying straight to her while the other cops read her dad his rights. Rio had gotten up by then, a small frown on his face as he stared at Desmond, as if he was trying to figure out what was wrong with Damian. She wondered if he knew Damian had a twin or if he was as in the dark as she'd been.

"Emily, are you okay?" Desmond asked as soon as he reached out, taking her by the shoulders and holding her in place while he looked her over. Bastian was right behind him, though his attention was divided between her and her dad, who was now being pulled into a sitting position with his hands cuffed behind him. It didn't escape her notice that *both* men had put themselves between her and her dad.

"I'm fine. He didn't touch me. Or anyone else." She smiled proudly.

Before either of them could say anything, the sound of a motorcycle revving got louder and louder, and this time when her heart leapt in her chest, she knew it was for the right reason.

Daddy's home.

Pulling away from Desmond, she darted around him and straight for the incoming motorcycle. Daddy stopped it well away from the crowd that parted to let her through.

"Emily!"

"I'm right here!" She pelted toward him, jumping into his arms for a hug, even though he'd barely gotten off the bike. Thankfully, she didn't knock him over, though it was a close call.

"Fuck." He squeezed her tightly against him, breathing in the scent of her with his nose against her neck.

There were a few titters and murmurs around them, and Emily realized they were making a bit of a scene, but she didn't care. If people now realized there was more to her staying in his trailer than just needing a place to live, oh well. They'd have figured it out eventually, anyway.

"Are you okay?"

"I'm fine, Da-Damian." Okay, so she might be fine with people knowing they were a couple, but she didn't want anyone overhearing her call him 'Daddy.'

That was their private thing, thank you.

"She's fine, Blake." Desmond came sauntering up behind them.

It was so weird hearing Damian called by his first name, even though he'd explained that he and Desmond both did it to each other just to get under the other's skin. Their whole relationship was a little weird. But then, she didn't have siblings. Maybe she just didn't understand.

"Thanks for being here." Daddy actually managed to sound sincere when he said it, and Desmond smiled at him.

"Of course. Bastian and I asked to be alerted if that asshole showed up anywhere near your girl. We wanted to be... around. Just in case."

Which was really very sweet of them. Letting go of Daddy, Emily spun around and threw her arms around Desmond, startling him so much, she almost knocked him over.

"Oh, um... there, there..." Desmond patted her shoulder awkwardly.

She snorted, shaking her head before letting him go. It only took a moment before Daddy was pulling her back against him, holding her close, as if he couldn't stand to let her go. She twisted around to look up at him.

"I'm sorry I made you leave work."

He hesitated, but only for a moment.

"Even if you had, that's not something to apologize for. But I wasn't actually at work, Sunshine." There was an odd note in his voice.

Emily twisted around so she could look at his face, frowning. He'd told her he was going to be at work all day, and it wasn't like him to lie. What was going on?

"You weren't?"

"No, I was visiting your mom." He dropped his hands from her, stepping back.

Sudden fear stabbed her through the heart. He'd gone to visit her mom? Without telling her? *Why?* And what had her mom said that made him look at her like this? Had she disapproved, even though she'd told Emily otherwise? Had she convinced him that they were too far apart in age? That they should break up?

Her heart pounded inside her chest, and the fear she felt was far more than when her dad had shown up today, than when he'd tried to grab her.

"Why?" She wanted to step toward him, but she didn't know if she should. If he was going to break up with her, she... she didn't know where she was going to go. Katrina's room was her only refuge, and it was still far too close to him.

He took a deep breath. "For this." He dropped to his knee, reaching into his pocket at the same time.

Emily's brain stuttered to a stop as all her expectations came to a screeching halt and reversed.

"Holy shit!" Desmond said, behind her.

"What is your brother doing?" That was Bastian.

At least, Emily assumed it was. She was having a little trouble thinking because her brain had turned to mushy chaos as she stared at Daddy lifting up a small black velvet box. Was that white noise in her brain or just all the things the neighbors were saying blurring together into a cacophony of indiscernible sound?

Meeting her gaze, Daddy popped open the lid.

DAMIAN

What the fuck are you doing, you old fool?

Going after what I want. Finally.

Now that he'd gotten into the habit, waiting felt too hard. He hadn't planned to do this at this moment. He couldn't have because he hadn't known this moment would happen. But it was, and he didn't want to lie to her, and... well, he couldn't wait.

She was staring at him, face pale, eyes wide, as if she didn't believe what she was seeing.

"Emily, I know this is really soon. I know it might even seem a little crazy. There are so many logical reasons not to do this, so many things working against us."

Getting depressing there, asshole, get to the good stuff. He cleared his throat.

"But at the end of the day, I love you. I think I've been in love with you for longer than I want to admit. And you don't have to say yes right now. I wouldn't blame you if you said no, but I wanted you to know where I stand. I love you, and I want to marry you, and—"

"Yes!" She cut him off, throwing herself forward and nearly knocking the box from his hand as she went down on her knees to wrap her arms around him. "Yes, I love you, and I want to marry you, and I don't care how crazy it is. We'll make it work."

Happiness rushed up inside him as cheers went up around them. There might be a few naysayers among the crowd, but it was obvious most of them were happy for him and Emily. And over her head, he could see Desmond glaring at everyone as if daring them to lodge a protest. Bastian came up beside him, watching and grinning as he slipped his fingers through Desmond's.

But they weren't who he wanted to be looking at.

Dipping his head, he swiftly pulled the ring out of the box and slipped it on Emily's finger before claiming her lips in a kiss, causing more cheering and whistling... and over the din, he could hear Don shouting.

"What the fuck? What the fuck is going on? What the fuck, Damian! Get your hands off my girl!"

Lifting his head, Damian met the gaze of his furious former friend. Don was flushed, enraged, and cuffed. His hands were behind his back, and his eyes were swollen and red. Damian knew at a glance Emily must have maced him.

Good girl.

"She's my girl now. And you are never going to come near her again." Wrapping his arms securely around Emily, Damian shifted so she couldn't see Don, and he couldn't see her. Bastian and Desmond immediately came up on either side of him, creating a wall of muscle.

"Fuck you!" Don screamed, struggling against the cops holding him. He managed to throw himself forward, as if he thought he was going to be able to crawl without the use of his arms. When the cops tried to pick him back up, he started kicking at them, still screaming.

"Oh, good," Bastian said mildly. "They'll be able to add on resisting arrest to the charges."

"And assaulting an officer," Desmond added when one of the kicks landed.

What a fucking tool. Damian could only shake his head before turning his back on Don and facing his Sunshine again.

"Come on, sweetheart, let's get inside. You don't need to see this."

"No, I really do," she said firmly, stepping forward to wedge herself between him and Desmond. "I want to see it. I deserve to see it. He's not my... not my dad. He's just my sperm donor, and I want to see him get exactly what he deserves."

Well, okay then.

He stood beside her as they watched her dad being wrestled into the cop car and driven away. He was part of the past.

Their future was together.

❧ 28 ❧

THE BIG ANNOUNCEMENT

DAMIAN

Seeing the ring on Emily's finger sent a thrill of satisfaction through Damian every time he looked at it. Satisfaction and possession. She was his, and the whole world was going to know it. All he wanted to do was celebrate.

First, though, they had to call Katrina.

"Are you freaking kidding me?" she screeched over the phone. Thankfully, it was on speaker rather than directly on either of their ears.

"No, that's why I texted you a picture of the ring." Emily glanced at him, still grinning despite Katrina's reaction.

"Geez, Dad, you went from moving at the pace of a glacier to suddenly hitting the fast-forward button."

Despite the teasing tone of her voice, he could hear her concern, and he understood it.

"Well, once I was willing to admit what I wanted, it didn't make sense to drag my feet. Plus, at my age..." He let his voice trail off, and his daughter groaned.

"Yes, exactly, at your age. Em, are you sure you want to tie yourself to this old man? I mean, I probably shouldn't be trying to convince you not to. I'm going to need help to wrestle him into a home in twenty years."

"Hey!" Damian was insulted. "Try... thirty. At least." Which would make Emily about his current age while he was in his eighties. "Or never, preferably."

"Well, I guess if you're married to her, then it will be her responsibility to wipe your butt. Okay, sold. Hi, New Mommy."

"I thought you weren't going to call me Mommy." Emily sighed, shaking her head. She shot Damian a bemused look. "I do get it. It's not like I don't think about these things for myself, but there are no guarantees in life. Look at my parents. They married appropriate people for their age, and now they're both going to be in jail. I could dump your dad, start dating a new guy my age tomorrow, and he could get hit by a bus. I'd rather have as many years together as we can than miss out on a single one because I'm afraid of a day that's decades away."

Damn. He stared back at her, feeling like his heart was swelling in his chest. He was so fucking lucky. And smart. Well, maybe dumb because he almost missed his chance, but he'd been smart enough to grab hold with both hands and put a ring on it now.

"I love you," he said.

"I love you, too."

The retching noise coming from the phone didn't ruin the moment as he kissed his fiancée.

"Ew, you're kissing, aren't you? I can hear it! Okay, I'm going now. I love you both, and I'm totally not grossed out by what's going on. Mostly. Byeeeeee." Katrina drew out the word, making Emily laugh against his lips as the phone call cut out.

Now that they had privacy, his cock—which had already been stiffening—surged to life. He wanted to fucking celebrate. Preferably by fucking.

"Oh!" She gasped against his lips as the kiss changed, deepening as he claimed her mouth, twisting her so he could move her back toward their bedroom. Truly *their* bedroom now. He was going to take care of her for the rest of his life.

Clinging to his neck, Emily kissed him back fiercely, letting him move her down the hall, one slow step after another to the bedroom. Clothing dropped to the floor as they moved, leaving a trail behind them. By the time they got into the room, they were mostly naked, and it only took Damian a moment to turn 'mostly' into 'completely.'

They tumbled onto the bed together, limbs wrapped around each other, tongues twining, until he got her exactly where he wanted her—on top of him. Flat on his back, he held her hips in place as she straddled his groin, the wet heat of her pussy rubbing against the underside of his cock.

Lifting her head, she looked down at him, heavy breasts swaying between them, the tips of her nipples brushing against his chest. Damian rocked upward, rubbing the length of his dick through her slick pussy lips and over her clit.

"Oh..." She shuddered, her lips parting on a soft gasp.

"Ride me, Sunshine. I want to see you bouncing on Daddy's cock."

She shifted atop him, leaning forward so she could angle herself correctly. They both moaned as he found her entrance, and she began to sink down on him. Damian ran his hands up her sides to her breasts, filling his palms with the soft flesh and pinching her nipples as she began to work herself onto his cock.

"Oh... Daddy..."

"That's it, Sunshine. Sit on Daddy's cock." His hips surged upward, impaling her, and she arched her back, throwing her head back as she moaned again. Sunk into her to the hilt, he could feel her pussy lips rubbing against his groin. He gave her nipples another hard pinch, using them to pull her forward for a kiss.

Her hands came to rest on his chest, ring flashing in the light, and he felt his balls tighten.

Fuck.

She was his.

All his.

And he was never going to let her go.

EMILY

Her thighs burned as she moved up and down on Daddy's cock, but she didn't stop. It felt too good. Kissing him, she squirmed, rubbing her nipples against the wiry hairs of his chest, the tender buds extra sensitive after all the pinching he'd been doing. Daddy's hands slid back down her sides to her ass, gripping her cheeks and using that to move her atop him, rocking her so her clit rubbed against his body.

Emily moaned again, her pussy clamping down around him as she shuddered with pleasure.

"Good girl. Fuck, you look so hot riding Daddy's cock."

She whimpered, squirming in place, then flexing her muscles to rise up and sink down again. Her breasts bounced as she moved up and down, keenly aware of his gaze as she moved atop him. It made her feel like a goddess. Moving faster, she rubbed her pussy against him, stimulating her clit every time she came to rest against his groin.

"Oh, please... Daddy! Oh, Daddy, I'm coming!" she cried out, shuddering.

His hands lifted her again, moving her on him, making her slide up and down his cock. Her pleasure mounted higher and higher, finally culminating in an explosion of hot ecstasy that had her writhing atop him, panting for breath.

But he wasn't done with her, his cock still rock-hard inside her, throbbing against her clenching channel.

"Keep going, Sunshine, don't stop," he ordered.

The stimulation was so intense, it was becoming painful as her tiny clit throbbed between them. It was too sensitive, too much. She *had* to stop, or at least get a small break from the intense sensations, the waves of agonizing ecstasy rippling through her.

She tried to lift up, but Daddy's hands gripped her tightly, holding her against him. Emily cried out again as she tried to squirm away, another wave of over-heated pleasure swamping her sense, pulling her under. No… she was actually going under, falling as Daddy rolled her over, so he was now the one on top. The suddenness of the switch amplified her disorientation, dizzying her. She screamed his name as he began to pound into her with rough, unyielding strokes.

The rapture exploding inside her was too much, dancing on the edge of pain and pleasure. She raked her nails down his chest as he folded her in half. With her legs spread, his body moving atop hers, rubbing against her pussy, there was nothing she could do but sob and take his cock, over and over again while the rampant ecstasy wrecked her from the inside out.

He pounded into her right through the spasms of her climax, pinning her to the bed and having his way with her while she screamed out as another orgasm assaulted her senses. Finally, he slammed home, groaning as he rubbed himself against her, throbbing inside her, and she could feel the hot spurts of liquid as they filled her.

Shuddering, she lay beneath him as he slowly relaxed on top of her, panting for breath and feeling so wonderfully safe and secure in his arms. When his head lifted so he could meet her gaze, she could see his love for her shining in his eyes.

"I love you, Sunshine."

"I love you, too, Daddy."

She couldn't wait to be his wife.

EPILOGUE

BRADEN

pplication Accepted.

Braden Elliott glared at the bright red letters scrawled across the top of the email he'd just opened. His application to the sex auction his club was supposedly running had just been accepted by the mystery person—or persons—who were using his club to legitimize their illegal activities.

How charitable of them.

Leaning back in his office chair, he sipped a glass of the exceptionally smooth whiskey he was taste testing for the bar. It, like the rest of his club, was extraordinary. The best of the best.

A secret online sex auction, especially one that

preyed on young virgins, did *not* meet those same requirements.

Not that the 'merchandise' wasn't top notch. At least from what he could see, considering most of the people putting themselves up for auction had chosen photos with their faces cropped out, or they'd opted to wear a mask. But the full body pics were certainly impressive, and a nice mix of everything from toned and athletic to muscular to full and curvy.

Still, he ran a respectable business. And if money ever exchanged hands for 'services provided' in his club, he preferred not to know about it. The idea of Club BDE sponsoring this kind of activity sat in his stomach like a lead weight.

The sooner they could figure out who was actually behind the auction so they could get it shut down, the better.

Sheer curiosity moved him to click out of the virgin auction to the other areas of the website. As he'd seen when Damian had first shown him the site, there were plenty of his members auctioning off various other "fantasies". Like Princess Raven— whose real name he knew to be Ivy—who was available for a whole list of fantasies, as long as her girlfriend was allowed to watch. Ivy and Cordelia had come to work for him years ago, and even before they'd officially become a couple they'd been so attached at the hip they'd affectionately earned the nickname "The Twins". Delia enjoyed watching others torment her poor little subbie as much as she enjoyed doing the deed herself, so it didn't really surprise him to see Ivy's listing.

Some of the others, however, did. Men and women alike who he knew were in committed, monogamous relationships, offering themselves up for various fantasies he knew for a fact their partners would never engage in.

Not that he wasn't sympathetic to their plight. He had his own needs, his own desires he'd learned to ignore over the years. Even at the club, he never indulged his more intimate fantasies. Truthfully, he rarely played at all anymore. He couldn't remember the last time he'd had a willing subbie up on a cross with his welts criss-crossing down her body from a thorough flogging. Or bent over a bench with the lines from his cane neatly stacked down her bottom and thighs.

Longer, still, since he'd had a woman to warm his bed.

It wasn't even that he had particularly unusual or depraved needs. Running a BDSM club on a daily basis, he'd seen enough to know he was nowhere near as sadistic as some of his friends. But he'd grown tired of scene after scene with the subs who all but fell at his feet. He'd come to realize over the past few years that what he really wanted was someone to match him, to challenge him. Someone who could walk confidently on his arm and match wits with the wealthy, educated types he tended to surround himself with. A graceful, sophisticated lady in public.

And Daddy's filthy little whore in private.

Such a woman, he'd yet to find.

Shaking off the melancholy settling over him, he stood and drained the rest of his drink as he made his way over to the one-way glass that allowed him to keep an eagle eye on his club while keeping his own privacy intact. He scanned the restaurant area on the upper floor briefly before shifting his attention to the lower floor, where the real action was happening.

To his relief, he recognized everyone who was playing tonight. Ever since he'd found out about that damned auction, it hadn't set well with him whenever he'd spotted someone he didn't know, especially those coming in as guests of his existing members. Newbies who wanted an actual membership had to undergo a thorough screening and in-person vetting process, so he wasn't as concerned about them.

But those who were brought in on guest passes had a much more surface-level background check. Which had never been a problem before, back when he'd trusted his members. Now, however...

Turning away from the windows, he made his way back to his desk and pressed the button on his phone that connected directly to the security room. "Martin. I need a word with you in my office, please."

"Uh, sure thing, boss. Be right there."

Settling back at his desk, he scrolled through the other fantasies, making mental notes as he waited for his head of security.

"Come in," he called at Martin's tentative knock.

"You wanted to see me?"

Tall and thin, with thick-framed glasses and a head of dark hair that always seemed in desperate need of a comb, Martin Hall looked every bit the computer geek Braden knew him to be. "I did. I want to change the process for screening guests. Until further notice, every application must be reviewed and approved by me once it has gone through our usual process."

Behind his glasses, Martin's eyes went wide. "*Every* application, boss?"

"Did I stutter, Martin?"

"Ah, no. I just...that's a lot of extra work for you to take on and I know how busy you are." Color rushed to the other man's face, giving him the look of a ripened tomato and making him seem much younger than he was. "I can take on the extra review, if you want."

"I appreciate the offer, but no. Just between us, there's something going on in my club and I want to keep a closer eye on things."

"What kind of something?"

It wasn't in Braden's nature to share his problems. Growing up with identical twin older brothers who'd once been thick as thieves, he'd learned to rely on himself at a young age. And now that Damian and Desmond seemed to hate each other, though nobody could really tell him *why*, he was reluctant to add his own drama to the mix. If it hadn't been Damian himself who'd brought the auction to his attention in the first place, he wouldn't have involved either of them until he'd gotten the situation sorted.

But he'd hired Martin because he trusted him. And because he'd passed the most intense background checks—including being tailed for a month by a private investigator—Braden could buy. So if he was going to confide in anyone, it would be Martin.

"What I am about to tell you does not leave this office. Understood?"

"Of course, boss."

"Someone is running an illegal auction, and using the club to make it seem legit. I'm working on finding out who the man behind the curtain is, but in the meantime, I want to keep a closer eye on who our members are bringing in. Maybe if they know I'm watching, they'll stop fucking around in my club."

"An auction? What kind of auction?"

"Sexual fantasies." He would keep the virgin part to himself for now, because it still made his stomach churn to think about it. "Which wouldn't be an issue except for the part where they're being paid for said sexual fantasies."

"Holy shit." Shaking his head, Martin let out a low whistle. "Do you want me to do some digging? If you send me the site, I can probably track them down."

"I appreciate the offer, but the police are already looking into it."

"That's good." Martin's smile flashed, a rare show of confidence. "But I'm better."

The laughter knocked some of the tension from Braden's shoulders. "If they don't find something soon, I may take you up on that. In the meantime, send any guest applications through me, and just keep a general eye on things for me."

"Got it, boss."

"Dismissed. Oh," he said as Martin turned to go. "Do me a favor and find Ivy and Cordelia, and send them to me. I believe they're working tonight."

"Sure thing."

Braden turned back to his computer as the door

shut behind Martin and clicked on Ivy's profile, studying the picture and the presented fantasies while he waited. It was, he was ashamed to admit, tempting to take them up on what they were offering, even if he had to pay for it. But they were committed to each other, and while he was certain he'd enjoy helping Cordelia torment her girl for an evening, it still wouldn't ease the pain of going home to a cold, empty bed.

As always, Cordelia only gave a cursory knock before bouncing into his office, her usual wide grin on her face. Blonde and curvy, with a bright and bubbly personality, she was every man's fantasy of the popular cheerleader. Right up until that man found himself on his knees begging for mercy. She was, without a doubt, one of the fiercest Dommes he'd ever come into contact with.

Behind her was Ivy, quiet and mysterious where Cordelia was loud and cheerful, though no less alluring for it. They were of a similar height, but where Delia was all soft curves, Ivy reminded him of the kind of elf you might find in a high fantasy. Slender and so pale she almost seemed ethereal.

More than one man had made the mistake of thinking quiet, reserved Ivy was the dominant partner, and Delia took great delight in making them pay for their assumptions.

Settling into one of his visitor's chairs, Delia pulled Ivy down into her lap, ignoring her girlfriend's brief struggle. A single look from her quelled Ivy's protests, and then Delia was all smiles again as she turned to Braden. "What's up, boss? Martin said you wanted to see us."

"I did." Gripping the top of his monitor, he turned the screen toward them, while he watched their faces for any sign of discomfort.

But there was none, though there was a hint of confusion in both of their expressions. It was, of course, Delia who spoke first. "Okay? What about it?"

"How did you find out about the auction?"

The confusion in Delia's expression intensified. "What do you mean? You told me about it."

Jaw clenched, he forced himself to take a deep breath through his nose before he said something he couldn't take back. "I certainly did not."

"Yes, you did," Delia insisted, her own temper flashing in her eyes. "You emailed me the information a few months ago, after we talked about me getting a raise. I thought it was kind of a dick move at the time, but after I saw the guaranteed bids, I realized it was a hell of a lot more money than you'd ever be able to pay me."

"Cordelia, I am telling you that I did not send you

that email. I just learned about this auction last week."

"And *I'm* telling you, the email came from your work account. That's the only reason I let Ivy sign up for it. You really think I'd risk my girl on some sketchy ass auction if it didn't come personally recommended by someone I trusted?"

Ivy snuggled closer to Delia, dark eyes wide in her pale face. "Mr. Elliott...if you're not the one running the auction, then who is?"

"I don't know." Turning the screen back to face him, Braden sent them both a determined glare. "But I'm damn sure going to find out."

Ⓐ

Braden will return in *Lottie* by Stella Moore, Book 2 of the Cherry Popping Daddies series.

ABOUT GOLDEN ANGEL

Golden Angel is a *USA Today* best-selling author of heart and bottom warming romance.

She is happily married, old enough to know better but still too young to care, and a big fan of happily-ever-afters, strong heroes and heroines, and sizzling chemistry.

When she's not writing, she can often be found on the couch reading, in front of her sewing machine making a new cosplay, hanging out with her friends, or wandering the Maryland Renaissance Fair.

www.goldenangelromance.com

bookbub.com/authors/golden-angel

goodreads.com/goldeniangel

facebook.com/GoldenAngelAuthor

instagram.com/goldeniangel

OTHER BOOKS BY GOLDEN ANGEL

CONTEMPORARY BDSM ROMANCE

Venus Rising Series (MFM Romance)

The Venus School

Venus Aspiring

Venus Desiring

Venus Transcendent

Venus Wedding

Venus Rising Box Set

Stronghold Doms Series

The Sassy Submissive

Taming the Tease

Mastering Lexie

Pieces of Stronghold

Breaking the Chain

Bound to the Past

Stripping the Sub

Tempting the Domme

Hardcore Vanilla

Steamy Stocking Stuffers

A Sassy Christmas

Entering Stronghold Box Set

Nights at Stronghold Box Set

Stronghold: Closing Time Box Set

Masters of Marquis Series

Bondage Buddies

Master Chef

Law & Disorder

Switch Play

Legally Bound

Shallow Submission

Hidden Away

Giant Tamer

Third Wheel

Dungeons & Doms Series

Dungeon Master

Dungeon Daddy

Dungeon Showdown

Daddies Everywhere

Chef Daddy

Foosball Daddies

Taco Daddy

Little Villain

HISTORICAL SPANKING ROMANCE

Domestic Discipline Quartet

Birching His Bride

Dealing With Discipline

Punishing His Ward

Claiming His Wife

The Domestic Discipline Quartet Box Set

Bridal Discipline Series

Philip's Rules

Gabrielle's Discipline

Lydia's Penance

Benedict's Commands

Arabella's Taming

Pride and Punishment Box Set

Commands and Consequences Box Set

Deception and Discipline

A Season for Treason

A Season for Scandal

A Season for Smugglers

A Season for Spies

Desire and Discipline

A Season for Bliss

A Season for Desire

A Season for Christmas

Bridgewater Brides

Their Harlot Bride

Standalone

Marriage Training

The Duke's Pursuit

Rogue Booty

SCI-FI ROMANCE

Tsenturion Masters Series with Lee Savino

Alien Captive

Alien Tribute

Alien Abduction

Standalone

Mated on Hades

SHIFTER ROMANCE

Big Bad Bunnies Series

Chasing His Bunny

Chasing His Squirrel

Chasing His Puma

Chasing His Polar Bear

Chasing His Honey Badger

Chasing Her Lion

Night of the Wild Stags

Chasing Tail Box Set

Chasing Tail... Again Box Set